A NOVEL BASED ON THE LIFE OF
LEONARDO DA VINCI

LEONARDO'S SECRET

Peter David Myers

THE
MENTORIS
PROJECT

Leonardo's Secret is a work of fiction. Some incidents, dialogue, and characters are products of the author's imagination and are not to be construed as real. Where real-life historical figures appear, the situations, incidents, and dialogue concerning those persons are based on or inspired by actual events. In all other respects, any resemblance to actual persons, living or dead, events, or locales is entirely coincidental.

Barbera Foundation, Inc.
P.O. Box 1019
Temple City, CA 91780

Copyright © 2018 Barbera Foundation, Inc.
Cover photo: iStock.com/exl01
Cover design: Suzanne Turpin

More information at www.mentorisproject.org

ISBN: 978-1-947431-09-6

Library of Congress Control Number: 2018933846

All rights reserved, which includes the right to reproduce this book or portions thereof in any form whatsoever except as provided by the U.S. Copyright Law. For information address Barbera Foundation, Inc.

All net proceeds from the sale of this book will be donated to Barbera Foundation, Inc. whose mission is to support educational initiatives that foster an appreciation of history and culture to encourage and inspire young people to create a stronger future.

The Mentoris Project is a series of novels and biographies about the lives of great Italians and Italian-Americans: men and women who have changed history through their contributions as scientists, inventors, explorers, thinkers, and creators. The Barbera Foundation sponsors this series in the hope that, like a mentor, each book will inspire the reader to discover how she or he can make a positive contribution to society.

*To Irv and Jeannette, who believed in me
and let me walk my own road.*

To Svetlana, who inspires me every day.

*And to those who seek to live with the truth
and create truth in all things.*

Contents

Foreword	i
Preface	v
Chapter One: The Dream	1
Chapter Two: Nonna	5
Chapter Three: Florence	13
Chapter Four: Verrocchio	17
Chapter Five: An Angel's Face	23
Chapter Six: Independence	31
Chapter Seven: The Adoration	37
Chapter Eight: Painting the Clock	47
Chapter Nine: Milan	57
Chapter Ten: Foothold	63
Chapter Eleven: Sforza	69
Chapter Twelve: Gran Cavallo	73
Chapter Thirteen: Corte Vecchia	83
Chapter Fourteen: The Last Supper	91
Chapter Fifteen: When Dreams End	105
Chapter Sixteen: Cesare Borgia	111
Chapter Seventeen: Mona Lisa	121
Chapter Eighteen: Slings and Arrows	127
Chapter Nineteen: The French Governor	135
Chapter Twenty: Francesco Melzi	145
Chapter Twenty-One: Between Florence and Milan	161
Chapter Twenty-Two: Farewell to a Friend	169
Chapter Twenty-Three: A Meeting with the Pope	177
Chapter Twenty-Four: The Nightmare	183
Chapter Twenty-Five: Seeking Peace	189

Chapter Twenty-Six: The French King	197
Chapter Twenty-Seven: From Italy to France	207
Chapter Twenty-Eight: Nothing	221
Acknowledgments	233
About the Author	236

Foreword

First and foremost, Mentor was a person. We tend to think of the word *mentor* as a noun (a mentor) or a verb (to mentor), but there is a very human dimension embedded in the term. Mentor appears in Homer's *Odyssey* as the old friend entrusted to care for Odysseus's household and his son Telemachus during the Trojan War. When years pass and Telemachus sets out to search for his missing father, the goddess Athena assumes the form of Mentor to accompany him. The human being welcomes a human form for counsel. From its very origins, becoming a mentor is a transcendent act; it carries with it something of the holy.

The Barbera Foundation's Mentoris Project sets out on an Athena-like mission: We hope the books that form this series will be an inspiration to all those who are seekers, to those of the twenty-first century who are on their own odysseys, trying to find enduring principles that will guide them to a spiritual home. The stories that comprise the series are all deeply human. These books dramatize the lives of great Italians and Italian-Americans whose stories bridge the ancient and the modern, taking many forms, just as Athena did, but always holding up a light for those living today.

Whether in novel form or traditional biography, these books plumb the individual characters of our heroes' journeys. The power of storytelling has always been to envelop the reader in a vivid and continuous dream, and to forge a link with the subject. Our goal is for that link to guide the reader home with a new inspiration.

What is a mentor? A guide, a moral compass, an inspiration. A friend who points you toward true north. We hope that the Mentoris Project will become that friend, and it will help us all transcend our daily lives with something that can only be called holy.

—Robert J. Barbera, President, Barbera Foundation
—Ken LaZebnik, Editor, The Mentoris Project

FOREWORD

As we approach the five hundredth anniversary of the death of Leonardo da Vinci, purveyors of information continually sow a proliferation of stories, art history books and articles, video games, television specials, films, and offerings of reattributions of works of art to the Renaissance master.

Worldwide interest in Leonardo is not surprising in a time when science overpowers the humanities and the public seeks out the fields of art and language, communication and history, and scholars move to link humanist interests to science. Today's use of the term "humanist" is misleading, but the traditional usage indicates those who study the gamut of fields from ancient languages and history to natural philosophy and mathematics, art and dance to rhetoric and geography—the various interests that kept Leonardo occupied for much of his life.

It is impossible to unpack all his unrelated interests and to concentrate fully on the many facets of his life as an artist. However, after reading *Leonardo's Secret*, you will undoubtedly know much about the milieu of the fifteenth-century artist, the techniques of a painter, and the temperament of the most famous artist-inventor of the Renaissance. Peter Myers's novel seeks to get at the heart of Leonardo's prime motivator, which is difficult to elucidate in someone so irritatingly complicated.

Myers arranges Leonardo's early life with his interest in nature that leads him to the wonders of the physical world and then to the intricacies of his mind and the higher thinking of math and astronomy, the nature of the cast shadows in painting and the play of light on solid forms. Not only do we learn about some of Leonardo's complex projects, but we immerse ourselves in his personal friendships—catalysts that help to explain his motivation and provide stimulation for his many intricate explorations of life on earth.

—Constance Moffatt, PhD
Professor of Art History

Preface

In researching this book, I came across video footage of tourists' and art lovers' faces as they looked at the *Mona Lisa*. One man's face was very telling. He appeared to be looking not at the painting, but into the mystery of himself.

A half-millennium has passed since Leonardo walked this earth, and still we plumb our own mysteries. For that very reason, among others, were we to pick the one man who, above all, ushered Europe into the modern age, Leonardo da Vinci would not be a surprising choice. His spirit of inquiry and observation was the cornerstone of science that imbued all he did and that has driven Western civilization to all its accomplishments.

Naturally, social, cultural, and philosophic forces—long in play as inevitable out-growths of the rise of towns in the Middle Ages—affected Leonardo during the High Renaissance, as they affected all thinkers and artists of his day. But it was how he directed and focused those forces that made him a permanent cultural icon and a venerated advocate of the supremacy of man and his mind as conqueror of the physical universe. The fact that Leonardo went further in the search to conquer even himself and his own mysteries—and, in his estimation, failed at the task—does not diminish his contributions or negate the insights he gave us through his art and his writings.

Embracing all disciplines and art forms, master of several, Leonardo not only intuited the future but also drew the society of his day into that future. His paintings inspired many generations of artists, including great masters such as Raphael. And his works still inspire us, and lead us inexorably forward, in the full confidence he had that man will *create* his own future rather than succumb to a self-created post-Apocalypse.

Leonardo's tragedy was that he was a searcher after peace, happiness, and a sort of meta-awareness for all men, but was starved for his own. Battered at every side by the same social forces that informed him, supported him, and yet restrained him, all he could manage was to create his masterpieces, do his research, and then write his barely readable notes backwards in the hope that someday, someone would find the ultimate truth he knew to be there and discoverable. To that, he gave his heart and soul.

I have written a book of fiction about Leonardo as possibly the only way I could understand him. In doing this, I tried to refrain from becoming mired down in the details of his life, and I took artistic license where I dared, believing that imagination is senior to facts. I did this to distill life, not to mirror it, which I feel is the purpose of all art. After all, art is what happens in life, minus the boring parts. Moreover, I tried never to lose sight of the big picture.

I salute you, Leonardo. You set the example for all of us who came after you. You never lost sight of the big picture, nor of the questions it inspires: Who are we? Why are we here? Where did we come from? Where do we go from here? Leonardo, you unselfishly gave your life and your masterworks to finding answers to those questions. Your efforts inspire all of us to this day. Thank you.

Los Angeles
June 2016

Chapter One

THE DREAM

In the full gleam of a summer afternoon in the year 1459, among the forests and foothills of Italian Tuscany, a handsome boy of seven lay in the weeds and grass by the side of a road. Leonardo, of the town of Vinci, was as motionless as the land around him that baked in the hot sun. His blue eyes were focused on a lizard that warmed itself on a rock, oblivious to the boy's slowly approaching hand.

The grass and weeds made Leonardo's skin itch, but he suppressed the urge to scratch. The constant trilling of the birds didn't distract him. His hand lunged like a bullet and snatched up the lizard.

Grinning with delight, Leonardo stood up and reached for his burlap sack. He held the lizard inches from his face and stared at it, fascinated. "Hello, Signore Lizard! You weren't quick enough today. Did the sun make you lazy?" He paused to take in his catch, examining its head and tail. "It's all right, my little friend. You're safe. I just want to study you. After that, I'll set you free."

Leonardo gently put the lizard in the sack and wiped the summer sweat from his brow. Intrigued by a myrtle plant, he snapped off a leafy stem and dropped it in his sack.

The voices of approaching children wafted on the breeze. Appearing around a bend in the road, three boys and a girl carried their own crudely woven burlap sacks, similar to Leonardo's, that had earlier held their lunches and now contained their lessons. They all saw Leonardo at once. He looked at them warily from the side of the road. A boy named Giorgio called out, "Look, it's the bastard child of Ser Piero the notary, hunting in the bushes again!" The other boys giggled.

Giorgio approached Leonardo with a phony smile. "Why don't you come to school with us, Leonardo? Oh, I forgot. You're a bastard. You can't go to school!" He looked at his friends to see how his punch line had landed. The boys laughed, enjoying the mockery of this strange child who kept to himself. But the girl was silent. She looked compassionately at Leonardo as he darted into the forest. The boys yelled and chanted after him, "*Eremita! Eremita!* Hermit! Hermit!"

At a safe distance from the road, Leonardo wiped his eyes. It wasn't the first time he had been teased, and he knew it wouldn't be the last. He sat at the foot of an old oak, put an arm around its trunk and leaned his head against it, as if it were a beloved uncle. Now content, he surveyed the peaceful forest and the soft green light that filtered through the leaves onto the forest floor. He felt a kinship with everything he saw. The birds didn't call him a hermit; they sang to him. The forest didn't laugh; it welcomed him with the open arms of its many branches. The forest was always there to accept and protect him.

Still, he wished he could go to school with the other children, wished they wouldn't make fun of him, and wished his father wouldn't largely ignore him, leaving Leonardo to his grandparents' care. Sometimes he felt very alone. He sighed like an adult resigned to life.

A songbird chirped above him in a nearby tree. "Why do you sing?" Leonardo asked aloud. It flew away and he laughed. "I want to fly like you!" he called after the bird. "I want to be free!" He felt better, having voiced his dream.

From farther away came the rat-a-tat of a woodpecker, stabbing its beak into the bark of a tree. Leonardo stood and followed the sound. He reached a tall pine where the woodpecker was hard at work.

Leonardo watched, totally absorbed. "Hello, bird!" he said. "Why do you do that?" The woodpecker plucked a grub from the bark. "So that's why!" Leonardo exclaimed. "You have to eat bugs all day to live!"

Leonardo drank in the sights, sounds, and smells of the forest. He looked up at the sun that shone through the trees. This was his true home. This was his schoolroom, where he could learn whatever he wanted. He spotted the bone of a small animal on the forest floor and picked it up.

After examining it closely, Leonardo added the bone to the collection in his sack. He did the same with a jagged-edged rock. At the edge of a meadow, he noticed a bee launching itself from a flower blossom. He plucked the blossom, studied it from every angle, and rubbed pollen between his fingers. "Why does the bee put your dust on its legs?" he asked the flower. "Does he eat it later?" He put the flower in the sack, along with a few leaves, oddly shaped twigs, and scraps of bark.

Later, walking past some bushes in the meadow, Leonardo saw a spider weaving a web between two branches. As he came closer, the spider sensed him and froze, suspended. Leonardo lay down in the soft grass and watched the spider, staying perfectly still. In a few moments, the spider resumed its task. Leonardo smiled, turned over on his back, and gazed at the sky.

Chapter Two

NONNA

On a summer afternoon the following year, Leonardo, now eight, sat on the forest floor and sketched a squirrel that rooted for food a few feet away.

"Pepino, you are such a pretty squirrel," he said. "Thank you for posing for me. Where is your girlfriend, Angelina, today? I want to draw her too." The squirrel pulled a chestnut from where he'd buried it and began gnawing at the shell. "Ah, you like chestnuts!" Leonardo exclaimed. "Tomorrow I will bring you some from home, and you can hide them for the winter."

The squirrel ran off with the chestnut. "Pepino! Where are you going?" Tucking his pencil and paper inside his sack, Leonardo followed the squirrel, which disappeared in thick underbrush. When he leaned down to peer through it, he was surprised to see the entrance to a cave.

Leonardo approached it warily, trying to see inside, and was met with darkness and silence. His face a mixture of curiosity and fear, he entered, moving slowly. His eyes became used to the darkness, but all he could see was the wall beside him. He slipped and fell, hitting his knee on the stone floor of the cave.

Moments later, screwing up his face in pain, Leonardo hobbled out of the cave. His right pants leg was torn open at the knee, which was skinned and bloody. Forgetting the squirrel, he limped toward home. Children from other households noticed his knee and asked about it, but he was silent. Gripping his sack, he entered his father's compound and walked toward his grandparents' house.

Lucia, Leonardo's grandmother—he affectionately called her Nonna—was slicing potatoes in the kitchen as Leonardo collapsed into a chair at the rough-hewn dining table. She shrieked at the sight of his bloodied knee.

"*Bambino! Madonna mia!* What happened to you? Are you all right?" She dropped her knife and potato and knelt on the floor in front of him. "What have you done to your knee?"

"It's nothing, Nonna. Just a scrape."

"Just a scrape, he says! What are we going to do with you? Sit still and don't move." She got up, dipped a rag in a pot of water that boiled on the hearth, and returned to his knee. He cried out as she applied the steaming rag.

"Are the other children making fun of you again?" Lucia wanted to know. "Did you get in a fight?"

"No, Nonna," Leonardo answered, wincing. "I was exploring and I tripped. It's nothing."

She pulled several clay jars full of herbs from a shelf and began grinding a mixture in a little hot water. "If your father were not always seeing clients away from the village, he wouldn't let you get into such mischief. Where did this happen?"

"I found a secret cave!" he said excitedly.

"So it's a cave this time? I hope this will teach you to stay out of such places. You might have surprised a wild boar and been gored to death, or been bitten by a badger or a snake!"

Leonardo knew how to play her. "Yes, Nonna, you're right," he said, making his face serious.

"You frighten me so when I think of you wandering the countryside alone!" his grandmother said. She took hold of his shoulders and put her face in front of his. "Leonardo, do you know how much Nonno and I love you?"

"Yes, Nonna." He paused. "But what about Papa?"

"Of course he loves you!"

Leonardo looked away. "I don't know."

"*Si, Bambino!* He loves you very much. But it's true he doesn't show it, and he's almost never here." She finished making her herbal paste and spooned some of it onto his knee. Then she wrapped the knee in a clean cloth. The paste stung a little, but Leonardo knew it was good because his Nonna had made it.

"*Finito!*" Lucia proclaimed. She stood, put her hands on her hips, and surveyed his knee as if its creation had been her accomplishment. "You could have been badly hurt, Leonino. Bleeding in a cave where the wolves would have found you before us. Don't go where you don't belong!"

Leonardo looked up at her with tear-filled eyes. "Where do I belong, Nonna?"

She embraced him. "*Bambino mio!* You belong right here. In my heart."

He basked in the warmth of his Nonna's embrace and the pleasant aroma of lamb and vegetable stew that simmered on the hearth. When her hug released the tension in his body, the thrill of exploration and new knowledge took hold of him once more.

"I had to look in the cave," he said, "or I wouldn't have known what was inside."

"*Basta*, you!"

"But it could have been something marvelous."

"There is nothing marvelous out there! Just trees and squirrels and dirt. You spend every afternoon in the forest and the hills and bring back useless objects." She pointed accusingly at the sack that bulged slightly with what she was sure were unpleasant contents.

"I have to study the animals and the plants!" he protested. "I want to learn all about them."

Lucia sighed. She had complained many times, to both her husband and her son, but had never managed to get the boy into a proper school. Her husband did what he could to teach him Latin and mathematics, but it wasn't enough. Without more education, Leonardo could never hope for any station in life higher than that of a notary, like his father.

She looked down sadly at her grandson. She knew there was greatness in him, and a powerful curiosity that couldn't and shouldn't be squelched. She regretted scolding him about the cave. She didn't want to dampen his spirit of adventure.

Lucia could never discuss what she saw in Leonardo with the men in the family—that he was destined for something more than obscurity in Vinci. Her husband and son had accepted their own lot in life. But Leonardo wasn't like them. Lucia often daydreamed about Leonardo leaving the village, making his way in the world, and becoming famous. For what, she didn't know, but she recognized his intelligence and creativity, and from that she spun a future. She brought her mind back from its wanderings and smiled at her grandson.

"*Mio bambino*, they won't let you into school. So you've made the world your schoolroom, haven't you?"

"*Sì*, Nonna. It's much more fun!"

"But nothing dangerous from now on. No more caves. Promise me!"

"No, Nonna, I can't," Leonardo said. At eight, he was already a young man of honor. He wouldn't promise because he knew that the next day might bring him another treacherous adventure, and he was game for it.

Lucia sighed. "You are too much for me, Leonino. I give up. But we'll see what happens when your father returns from Florence."

She cleaned up the remains of the herbs and went back to her potatoes. Leonardo walked toward the door.

"Dinner will be ready soon," she said. "Where are you going?"

"To sit outside, Nonna."

She smiled and sliced a potato.

Leonardo sat idly on the front stoop of the house. He was bored. He watched a sheepdog puppy playing with its mother. Then he saw Lucio, the beekeeper, coming down the path with a cart full of honey deliveries in glass jars.

Lucio hailed him as he drew close. "*Ciao*, Leonardo! How are you today?" He noticed the bandage on Leonardo's knee. "What happened to you, little one?" Leonardo shrugged.

Lucio approached, knelt down, and pulled away part of the bandage to examine the minor wound. "That's not too bad. I think you'll live." He took a honey jar from his cart and began applying honey to the wound.

Leonardo protested, "Nonna already did that!"

"That's herb paste, but you can't beat honey for stopping *infezione*," Lucio said.

Leonardo winced a little, as his knee was still tender. "Can you put a lot on?" he asked.

Lucio laughed. "So you can eat some of it, eh?" Leonardo laughed with him.

Lucio finished with the honey and replaced the bandage. He took a rag, wrapped a piece of honeycomb, and handed the gift to Leonardo. "And this is to eat."

Leonardo thanked him and asked, "Lucio, how do bees make honey?" He was as thirsty for knowledge as he was hungry for honey.

"Who knows?" Lucio said, pointing upward. "Those things are best left to God."

Leonardo looked up and searched the sky. "Where is God? I don't see him."

"Leonardo, my boy, you ask too many questions."

"Too many for what?"

Lucio was at a loss for words.

That night, in Leonardo's room, a lit candle illuminated a small table that held some of the items Leonardo had picked up in the forest. Moonlight shone through the window onto to the walls and the furniture. From outside came the sounds of the night. Crickets chirped, a dog howled, and somewhere, someone played a lute—badly. Oblivious to all this, Leonardo sketched an animal bone on a piece of paper. He turned the bone at different angles to understand its three-dimensionality.

Hanging on the wall beside his crude bed were ambitious but imperfect sketches of trees, plants, flowers, animals, and landscapes. A short length of pig intestine hung from another wall, blown up like a balloon, a funny face drawn on it in ink. A hat with a feather hung from a nail. Waiting in a corner was Leonardo's backlog: several sacks full of what he viewed as life's mysteries, yet to be plumbed. A lizard climbed out of one and hid in a corner.

Finished with his sketch, Leonardo sat back, yawned, smiled, and admired the moon. "*Que bella luna,*" he said to himself. He climbed into bed and went to sleep.

Chapter Three

FLORENCE

Years went by, and Leonardo became a handsome youth of fifteen. On a sunny day in 1467, he stood with his father at the crest of a hill overlooking Florence. The city sparkled in the afternoon sun. The river Arno curved sensuously, caressing its banks as it flowed through the middle of town.

Leonardo felt that this day would change his life. All his senses were at their height. He noticed everything: the intense blue of the sky, the breeze on his cheek, the birds singing in the trees. His heart swelled at the prospect of what the future might bring.

His father, Piero, had brought him to Florence partly for his own notary business, and partly with a view to accomplishing a specific goal: giving Leonardo a start in life. In that moment, Leonardo felt he was truly and fully his father's son. He pushed from his mind any thought that their closeness might be only temporary.

A rarity in a country torn by incessant wars between city-states, Florence was resplendent in its economic stability. Its painted walls glowed in mellow contentment, and its uniformly red-tiled roofs seemed to hold the promise of beautiful adventures.

To Leonardo, Florence was a wondrous spectacle, a treasure chest full of dreams. Here, his hard work—by now, he had created thousands of drawings—would come to fruition. Here, he would pursue the life of an artist, someone whose talent was needed and wanted by wealthy patrons and well-funded clergymen. Here, he could continue his quest to know everything there was to know.

"Here, I can breathe," he thought to himself. "No one will taunt me for my illegitimate birth, or my lack of formal education."

As for Piero, he would do what he could to secure a future for his son. Although he never married Leonardo's mother, a servant girl, he felt responsible for Leonardo. Maybe the boy could be an artist after all. His chances were certainly better in Florence than in Vinci.

The two returned to the wagon that held all of Leonardo's worldly possessions. Piero shook the reins, and the mule plodded down the trail toward the city. He chose his words carefully, masking his emotions. "As you know, Leonardo, I have a sizable clientele here as a notary. Perhaps you can make a living here as well, through your drawing."

Leonardo smiled. "Thank you, Papa, for bringing me on this trip with you. I won't forget your kindness."

"To enter the painters' guild should be your aim," Piero continued briskly. "Your talent needs guidance. I pray that my friend and client, Verrocchio, will take you as an apprentice. He is a well-respected master in Florence."

"I'll be worthy of your favor, Papa. Where will we live?"

"I've rented a house across the piazza from the Hall of the Five Hundred, where the leaders of Florence meet."

Leonardo was silent. Piero glanced sideways at him. "Do you already miss the woods and the fields?" he asked.

"No, Papa," Leonardo said. "I'll find my place here."

When they reached the city gates, the guards, who knew Piero, let them enter without any formalities. Slowly, they made their way through throngs of pedestrians, wagons, hawkers, food stalls, priests, and beggars. The market stalls contained animals of every kind, shape, and size. Leonardo was fascinated by the mélange of sights, sounds, smells, and tableaux, a never-ending stream of human activity. Wanting to draw everything, he reached for his sketchbook, then remembered it was packed away in the wagon behind him. He vowed to store everything in his mind for later.

Piero smiled at his son's fascination. "A little different than Vinci, eh?"

Thrilled, Leonardo could only utter, "*Certo!*"

Chapter Four

VERROCCHIO

Piero and Leonardo stood before one of the most famous art studios in Florence, the source of works that drew clients from all over Europe and even Russia. They were in a part of the city that was home to numerous workshops and studios of artists and craftsmen. Here there were no fetid odors of animals or rotting produce.

The studio belonged to Andrea del Verrocchio, an artist in his mid-thirties and already famous as a painter, sculptor, and goldsmith. He had been nicknamed Verrocchio ("true eye") by an admiring patron. His real name, known to Piero, his notary, was Andrea di Michele di Francesco de' Cioni. The wags of Florence joked that the artist's real name was too much of a mouthful for the patron. The nickname let the patron save considerable breath when introducing the artist at parties.

In the uniquely mellow sunshine of a Tuscan afternoon, apprentices stood in a fenced-off yard in front of the studio. They worked diligently on marble busts, figures, and a few reliefs. Leonardo was impressed with the variety, quantity, and quality of their output. As the apprentices chiseled, chips flew off the blocks, landed on the flagstones, and were swept up by an assistant.

Two apprentices were taking a break from their labors. They talked and laughed as they ate bread and cheese and drank wine. One of them recognized Piero and smiled.

"*Ciao*, Ser Piero! You came from Vinci today?"

"*Ciao*, Aristotele!" Piero answered. "Yes, we have just arrived." With something resembling pride, he added, "This is my son, Leonardo. Is your master inside?"

"*Si, certo!* I will tell him you're here. Would you like some bread and cheese?"

"No, *grazie*," Piero said.

Aristotele looked at Leonardo. "And you?"

Leonardo nodded. "Yes, please. I'm hungry."

Aristotele tore off a chunk of dark bread, added a slice of mozzarella, and handed it to Leonardo. The two shook hands.

"Your name is Aristotele?" Leonardo said. "Your parents had great hopes, eh?"

The apprentice laughed. "I'm afraid I've disappointed them." He turned to fetch his master.

Newcomers to Verrocchio's studio were put off at first by his seemingly aloof manner. Once they were introduced to him, they found him to be warm and cordial with a hint of familiarity—qualities that were useful in gaining new clientele.

When a scowling face appeared at the studio's entrance, Leonardo was more curious than wary. Growing up in Vinci, he had observed many inconsistencies in human behavior. As Piero and Verrocchio embraced and his father made the introductions, Leonardo thought that someone like Verrocchio was preferable to an overly friendly stranger who later turned out to be a backstabber.

Verrocchio's large, bustling studio was a source of wonder to Leonardo. Everywhere he looked, apprentices were busy with paintings, sculptures, and gold and brass ornaments. They glanced at him briefly, then went back to work.

Verrocchio saw the look in Leonardo's eyes. To Piero, he said, "What have we here? The next generation of notaries?"

Without waiting for his father to reply, Leonardo spoke up. "I'm a painter." In truth, he aspired to be a painter. So far, he had only made drawings. He knew nothing about painting.

"I see," Verrocchio said. "But are you a hard worker? There are many in Florence who call themselves painters but don't have enough self-discipline to paint a block of wood."

Leonardo felt his self-confidence waver. Aristotele, who had come inside to watch, winked at him. Leonardo said to Verrocchio, "Give me a block of wood and I will show you."

Verrocchio laughed. Piero scolded his son, "Don't bother him with such things."

But Verrocchio looked approvingly at Leonardo and then at his father. "Your son has spirit, even if he turns out to have no talent."

"He has both, my friend. He almost scared me to death one day with a mask of Medusa he created. Andrea, I am hoping you might take him as an apprentice."

Verrocchio seemed to consider Piero's request, as if he hadn't known it was coming. "Hmmm," he said, scratching his chin. "It seems you can frighten people, young man, but can you also give them pleasure by making things of beauty?"

"I like that much better," Leonardo said.

"Then there is some hope for you," Verrocchio replied. To Piero, he said, "I welcome your son as my apprentice." He turned back to Leonardo. "And you, my young friend, get ready for some long, hard work and little pay."

Verrocchio took them back to his office, where he kept a fine brandy for special occasions.

Leonardo learned fast. In two years, he absorbed and applied every technique and principle that had made Verrocchio a success in the Florentine art world. He moved through the studio, observing, copying, improving upon, and grasping everything, just as he had swept through the forests of Vinci, learning all the forest had to offer.

On any given day, Leonardo could be found mixing paints (and experimenting with new mixtures), chiseling marble, painting a minor figure in a crowd scene, sketching another apprentice as he worked, painting the rocks in the background of an altarpiece, being instructed on a painting detail by another apprentice, or being coached by Verrocchio himself on the background face in a portrait. Later, when Leonardo was a senior apprentice, the master allowed him to paint the robes in a portrait of a notable clergyman. Eventually, he had Leonardo paint more of the secondary faces in his commissions.

Almost from the start, a mutual admiration and trust existed between apprentice and master. Often, at the end of a day's work, the two retired to Verrocchio's office for brandy and conversation. Verrocchio came to recognize the depth and sharpness of Leonardo's mind. Nothing was beyond the scope of the young man's inquiry. He wanted to know how everything worked. The more he read, the more he wanted to know, and the more questions he asked—questions Verrocchio could not begin to answer.

Sometimes, late at night, Verrocchio would marvel at Leonardo's excited eyes as he rattled off questions or theories. Scientific, philosophical, religious, aesthetic: they flowed from him like a rushing river.

"This young man has completely eclipsed me in thought and word," Verrocchio mused to himself one day. "Soon, with his paintings, he will eclipse me in deed as well. He will be the greatest artist ever produced on the Italian peninsula. Art students will come to my studio not to view my work but to ask, 'Your apprentice, Leonardo da Vinci…what was he like?'"

Verrocchio knew it was just a matter of time before Leonardo left the nest to which his notary and friend Piero had led him. A lesser person would have been jealous of Leonardo, or might have attempted to squelch his talent, but Verrocchio wasn't like that.

One night, in an attempt to forestall the inevitable, he offered Leonardo a full partnership in his studio.

"Maestro, you honor me greatly," Leonardo replied. "But I fear I owe you too much already for what you have taught me. I could never accept this."

Verrocchio sighed. "All right. Let's have another drink. But I won't give up so easily."

Chapter Five

AN ANGEL'S FACE

More years passed. One day, Leonardo knelt on the floor of Verrocchio's studio, putting the finishing touches on the face of an angel. In fact, they were the finishing touches on the whole painting, Verrocchio's *Baptism of Christ*. Other apprentices, including Aristotele, gathered around. Reverently, they watched him make a delicate line with a very thin brush. Leonardo's freehand draftsmanship was impeccable.

Verrocchio had painted Christ standing in a narrow stream, his feet visible through a few inches of water. But even that skill was trumped by Leonardo's young angel, whose right cheek seemed to glow with an inner light as she glanced up at Jesus.

Aristotele smiled and rushed off toward Verrocchio's office. He bounded inside. Verrocchio looked up from some paperwork. "Maestro! Come and see what Leonardo has done with the angel!"

Verrocchio followed him to the group of apprentices who surrounded Leonardo. He nudged his way past them to stand directly behind Leonardo, who looked up at him, smiled, and went back to work. Leonardo put a tiny dab of paint on the angel's hair. Then he stood and stepped back to give Verrocchio a view of the piece. "I think it's finished. What do you think?"

Verrocchio looked at the painting and was so touched by Leonardo's angel face that he didn't know whether to laugh or cry. He stepped back and sat down on a nearby chair. The apprentices looked concerned for him. "No, it's all right," he said. "I'm all right."

"Maestro, what's wrong?" Leonardo asked. "Did I ruin your painting?" Verrocchio let loose with a flood of laughter and tears, confusing everyone. Finally, calming himself, he stood up and approached the painting again. He looked long and hard at the angel's face. There was an initial flash of jealousy in his expression, followed by another, more complicated emotion. Still speechless, he appeared to hold back more tears.

"You don't like it?" Leonardo asked.

"On the contrary. I'm devastated that a youth in his twenties knows more about painting than I do." Gasps of surprise were heard. "The angel breathes!" Verrocchio continued. "She's like flesh and blood! Her presence strikes me with such force that it's hard to bear." He paused.

"Leonardo, you have made her face shine with a light that we have not seen before. I think it is you who have come from heaven to guide us."

What Verrocchio had said technically amounted to heresy, but the apprentices let that pass. Everyone looked at Leonardo, who shrugged.

"There's nothing so spectacular about it, really. An angel's face would, necessarily, emanate the light of the spirit. Am I wrong?"

No one had ever said that so simply before, with such clarity. All the apprentices shook their heads, as if Leonardo's rhetorical question demanded an answer.

Verrocchio smiled. The ease with which Leonardo dismissed his own genius astounded him. "Maybe, someday, we shall all have that same light," he offered.

Panicked thoughts of *real* heresy raced through the apprentices' minds. Verrocchio wondered to himself, "Is there no end to the profundities of this backwoods creature?" Then he said, "Leonardo, your contribution is so powerful that it almost disrupts the unity of the piece."

The apprentices took this to mean that the maestro felt challenged. An uneasy silence descended. Verrocchio continued. "Almost—but not quite." Relieved laughter.

Verrocchio approached Leonardo. The feeling in the room shifted to anticipation.

"You are my partner now, Leonardo," Verrocchio said quietly but firmly.

"But Maestro, I cannot—"

"My son, I'm afraid you must. In the future, all painting commissions will be done under your brush or under your direction, as I will not paint again. Now, I can finally focus on my favorite things, sculpture and goldsmithing."

He put his hand out to shake Leonardo's, but the young man had just sat down and was too overwhelmed to stand.

"Ser Andrea, I am honored and very grateful."

"Stand up, young genius!" Verrocchio commanded. Leonardo obliged, and Verrocchio gave him a congratulatory hug. Everyone else clapped and cheered.

∽

Evening found Leonardo at a table full of lively apprentices, all in their teens and twenties. Glasses, half-empty bottles of wine, piles of bread, dishes of pasta, vegetables, cheeses and fruits, and the remains of a huge roast mutton littered the table while Leonardo and his friends joked and laughed. One played a flute with passable skill.

Sandro Botticelli, handsome and a little arrogant, sat at one end of the table, felt his bulging stomach, and cried out, "*Ay, amici*, I will not eat again for a week!" Another apprentice teased, "It's just as well, Botticelli, you haven't worked on a commission for a month!" Laughter boomed around the table.

"Don't be mean to Sandro, boys," Leonardo admonished them. "He's saving his talents for the Medicis." This was followed by several guffaws.

Pietro Perugino, who was chunky, stern, but open-minded, commented on Botticelli's plight. "That's all right. Every painter must have his day before the ultimate arbiters of taste in Florence."

"And how do they taste, Perugino?" a wag wanted to know.

More laughter was interrupted by Aristotele, who raised his glass. "And now, to Ser Leonardo da Vinci, the new partner of the studio!"

Botticelli added, "To another boss!" Everyone raised their glasses.

"Thank you, Aristotele, but leave off the Ser," Leonardo said.

"No false modesty, Leonardo. We are witnessing a new light shining in Florence."

Perugino added, "Let's hope it won't blind us."

"*Certo!*" Botticelli agreed. "If we were blind, we could never appreciate the beauty of his paintings."

Yet more laughter, and the glasses were refilled.

"Leonardo, will you play for us on your viol?" Botticelli asked.

"No, but I'll play for you on my lute." He bent down and took a lute from a case. He tuned it quickly and played a Tuscan folk song.

An hour later, they were still drinking. One of their number had passed out, the side of his face resting in a plate of pasta. Botticelli painted dots on his face with red sauce.

"You should have pity on the poor soul, who will surely be embarrassed tomorrow," Leonardo said.

Aristotele, drunk, waxed philosophical, "Ah, the soul. The soul! Ultimately, the soul is in God's hands, and we cannot know anything about it until we get to heaven."

Botticelli added, "*If* the soul goes to heaven, and not the other place."

"And *if* there is a soul at all," Perugino opined. "That, I doubt."

"But *if* the soul has an existence independent of the body, might it not also be independent of God?" Botticelli wondered.

"If one were to follow your proposition, Sandro, then when the body dies, the soul could go where it pleases, which is ridiculous," Aristotele said. "The church teaches us that the soul can only go to heaven or hell, or, temporarily, to purgatory."

Perugino put his glass down loudly. "Has any one of you seen a soul? Can you tell me where it is?" He looked at each person at the table. All were silent. One shrugged. Perugino continued, "Leonardo, what do you feel the soul is, and where is it, do you think?"

All eyes turned to Leonardo.

"It's a fascinating subject," he began. "Unfortunately, I doubt that I have the intelligence to address it." This was met with scoffs and groans.

"Oh, come on, Leonardo!" Perugino said impatiently.

"All right," Leonardo said. "Whatever the soul is, it must be a divine thing, don't you think?"

"The soul is God's responsibility," Aristotele declared. "We cannot know more, and we should leave it at that."

Later, Leonardo took a leisurely walk with Aristotele. He had not gotten drunk with the rest of them, and Aristotele had sobered up in the night air.

"Why are you so silent?" Aristotele wanted to know.

"The best paintings I have seen have all dealt with the soul," Leonardo said. "The question is, why?"

"Other than what we know from the Bible and the catechism, the soul is a mystery and probably always will be," Aristotele answered impatiently. He was tired of serious talk.

"I think the riddle is solvable," Leonardo said. "I just want to *know*, as any of us do. I've always felt there is something…a 'me,' a self…that is not—" Leonardo indicated his body—"this." He paused. "But then, what is it? Don't you want to know, Aristotele?"

"You go too far, Leonardo," Aristotele said gently.

"Possibly. But I share this with you only because you're my dearest friend."

"*Grazie*. You're mine as well. But the church will never condone such an inquiry."

"Nor can they squelch the desire to know that is natural to man."

Aristotele shook his head. "This is a question that has confounded even the greatest philosophers."

"Nonetheless, a secret, if it is a secret, can be discovered."

"But how do you expect to find what they could not?"

Leonardo smiled, "They weren't painters."

"So?"

"To be a painter, one must be a great observer not only of people, but all of nature. We are a small part of the natural world, but a painter distills the images of life into valuable truths—or he isn't a painter."

"Leonardo, don't share this with anyone. The church treats such ideas as heresy." Aristotele sighed. "You were lucky to come from the countryside and be admitted to Verrocchio's studio. And luckier still to be made a partner. But you deserved it, and you will find great success—unless you say the wrong thing to the wrong people."

Aristotele looked his friend in the eye. "Don't ruin your success at Verrocchio's," he warned. "The maestro is very loyal to the church."

Chapter Six

INDEPENDENCE

Leonardo, Botticelli, and Perugino emerged from the doorway of an ornate building on Via Firenze. A sign above the doorway read "The Confraternity of Saint Luke," an organization that served informally as the painters' guild. Without membership in this organization, which dated back to 1349, a painter would have a hard time securing commissions. Leonardo was now a member, and he could secure his own commissions if he chose. He had the bright eyes of someone who had just been empowered.

He read an official-looking scroll as he walked with his friends. Botticelli said, "Congratulations, you're one of us!"

Perugino joked, "Botticelli, is there any chance for you and I to get commissions now?"

Botticelli answered, "With Leonardo in the guild? It's hopeless." They laughed.

Botticelli indicated Leonardo. "Maybe we should simply dispose of him in the Arno on a dark, moonless night."

Perugino added, "Splendid idea! You get a large burlap sack. I have a friend with a horse and cart."

Aristotele approached from a side street. To Leonardo, he said, "Sorry I'm late. Are you accepted?" Leonardo held up the scroll.

"Of course he's accepted!" Perugino exclaimed. "He's the best painter in Florence."

"Excepting myself, of course," Botticelli said.

"I'm simply an observer," Leonardo protested.

"Fine, then let's observe a good bottle of wine."

Leonardo begged off. "Another time, my friends." He turned to Aristotele, "Walk with me on the way home, will you?"

Moments later, the two conversed on another street lined with milliners' shops.

"But you are an integral part of Verrocchio's studio!" Aristotele protested. "He's bringing you with him to Pistoia to help with the commission at the Cathedral."

Leonardo replied, "And he is also bringing Lorenzo di Credi, who is advanced enough now that he could easily replace me."

Aristotele scoffed. "As if anyone could replace you."

"I'm already in my twenties, yet I have finished no artworks made solely by myself. I must move on, Aristotele. Not just to paint, but also to explore other creative, scientific, and philosophical disciplines."

"Disciplines? What do you want to learn?"

"I want to know everything it is possible to know."

"We have had this sort of discussion before," Aristotele said. "There are some things it is not possible to know."

"If a question can be asked, observation can provide the answer."

"Someday, you'll change your mind about this."

Leonardo calmly replied, "A sailor whose eye is fixed to a star does not change his mind."

∼

In the Cathedral of Pistoia, a town about twenty miles from Florence, Leonardo, Verrocchio, and Lorenzo di Credi finished their work for the day. They put away their painting supplies and cleaned their spaces. Leonardo covered his work with a tarp.

"Lorenzo, go ahead to the house," Verrocchio said, wiping his hands with a rag. "Leonardo, stay behind." Credi looked questioningly at the maestro, then nodded and left.

Verrocchio turned to Leonardo. "Are you feeling all right?"

"I'm very fit, thank you. Why?"

"I brought two very capable assistants with me for this commission. But, frankly, your work does not show your usual passion. Is something wrong with your health?"

Leonardo gathered his thoughts before speaking. "It's not my health, Andrea. It's my desire to establish my own studio."

Verrocchio nodded sadly. "It is time, isn't it?"

"I'm betraying you by leaving, aren't I?"

"Please, none of that!" Verrocchio responded. "You're in your prime. I would do the same thing." He saw the distraught look on Leonardo's face and rushed to comfort him. "Don't worry about the studio. Lorenzo will fill the gap."

Despite Verrocchio's words, Leonardo still felt guilty. He owed a tremendous amount to this man who had given him the technical expertise he needed to succeed. Leonardo's mind drifted back to the day his father had brought him to the studio. He imagined his fifteen-year-old self, gazing everywhere with wonder. And wasn't there some talk about painting wood blocks? He returned to the present.

"Thank you for understanding, Maestro Andrea."

"It's you who are the maestro," Verrocchio said. "Go and make your mark in Florence. And whatever you need—money, an assistant to borrow—just ask."

Leonardo embraced him. Verrocchio was truly an unselfish friend.

Leonardo secured a modest studio on a quiet side street in a humble section of Florence and hired a young assistant named Paolo. Within a week, he had set up several easels, drawing tables, paints, and tools. His lute and viol hung from one wall. He settled in.

One day, Leonardo sat at a table, studying a drawing of a bird's wing he had just completed. He compared it with the real wing on the body of a dead bird he found in an alley.

A knock came at the door. Leonardo called out, "*Vieni!*"

A messenger in his mid-teens entered and took off his hat. "Ser Leonardo, I have a letter from a priest in the Piazza della Signoria." Leonardo took the letter, thanked the boy, and handed him a coin.

"From the Chapel of Saint Bernard in the Piazza della Signoria," he announced to Paolo. He opened the letter, read it, and smiled.

A few days later, Leonardo sat in a pew in St. Bernard's. Looking dejected, he eyed an oddly shaped section of a wall to the left of the altar. Its lower right corner had been abruptly cut off to accommodate an arched doorway. Aristotele entered the chapel, sat down beside Leonardo, and studied the open sketchbook on his friend's lap. He saw a sketch of the Virgin and Child.

"Paolo told me I would find you here," Aristotele said. "Congratulations! Where does the painting go? And why the sad face?"

Leonardo grunted an acknowledgment, then pointed to the left of the altar.

"There?" Aristotele said, not believing his eyes.

"It's hopeless," Leonardo groaned. "Not only is the lower right corner cut off, but the light is uneven. A normal painting will look off balance. Any attempt I make will ruin my reputation as a painter. I saw that wall yesterday, and I couldn't sleep last night."

"Don't worry," Aristotele said, as lightly as he could. "You have no reputation yet to ruin."

Leonardo shrugged, then smiled. "You are a true friend, because you are an honest friend." He stood. "Lunch?" Aristotele smiled back, and the two men stood and walked toward the door.

The St. Bernard chapel was Leonardo's first commission, but it was a recipe for failure, and he shrank from it. He never even started it. Antonio del Pollaiuolo had originally been given the commission, but he abandoned it. After Leonardo, Domenico Ghirlandaio inherited the task. He also gave up. As Leonardo often told himself, "An unhealthy tree will bear no fruit."

Chapter Seven

THE ADORATION

Several months later, Leonardo was comfortably working on a commission in a building with a much better wall space. Paolo, who had been mixing paints, watched his master put the finishing touches on a Madonna and Child in which Mary held out a flower for baby Jesus to examine. A monk approached and studied the almost completed painting.

"It's beautiful, Leonardo," he said. "I have never seen anything like it."

Leonardo thanked him. "I have my own way of looking at Mary," he explained. "As a woman and a mother, rather than a figure on a throne. I hope I have succeeded in symbolizing God's love through Mary's love for Jesus."

The monk said admiringly, "You have."

"Someday, I hope to reveal the secrets of life," Leonardo mused aloud. "And even the secrets of soul. Through a hand gesture, like this one." He pointed to Mary's hand that offered a flower to her son. "Or through a smile." His Mary was smiling. The monk didn't know what to say.

∽

In March of 1481, Leonardo was sketching a large animal bone as his father, Piero, entered the studio. The notary surveyed the space and his son, absorbed in a bone.

"Good morning, Leonardo," Piero said, trying not to sound too disapproving.

"Hello, Father!" Leonardo answered, looking up from his sketch.

Piero sat in a nearby chair. "I have good news, but then I must hurry to a client's house. I have persuaded the monastery of San Donato a Scopeto to give you a commission. You will do a great painting of Mary, Jesus, and the Magi, and not for a side chapel, but for the main altar!"

Leonardo's face brightened. "That is wonderful news!"

"From now on, you won't have to study bones, stars, and birds' wings."

"But Father, I must know bone structure as a painter. And I study how birds fly. With the right sort of apparatus, man can fly too."

"You know how I feel about that fantasy of yours," Piero replied. "I'm bringing you something from the real world. But you won't be paid to start work. You'll be compensated later, with a one-third ownership of a small estate in Val d'Elsa. You must contribute one hundred fifty florins to the estate heiress's marriage dowry, and also pay for your own paint and gold leaf."

Leonardo strove to stay calm. "Father, what sort of deal is this?"

"A deal that will further your reputation in Florence. The world will see that you can do a painting in the grand style, two-and-a-half meters across! You're sure to get more commissions as a result."

Leonardo sighed. He resigned himself to doing the work, if only out of love for his father.

In April, Leonardo knelt on the floor of his studio. He was sketching a cartoon, a full-size study for his painting, on a very large sheet of paper. Many other large sketches and studies lay on the floor nearby. Behind him was a wooden board, eight feet square, on which an undercoating had already been painted.

A horse and wagon pulled up outside. Moments later, a monk from San Donato entered without knocking. His eyes fixed on Leonardo, completely absorbed in his work. The monk looked in dismay at the blank white board and the sketches on the floor.

"Good day, Ser Leonardo," he said.

"Good morning, Father," Leonardo said, rising to his feet. "As you can see, I'm working on your commission."

"And yet, you have not even finished the cartoon."

"I never attach the final sketch to the working surface, let alone apply the paint, until I feel I have mastered the subject," Leonardo explained.

"But others before you have long since mastered it," the monk retorted. "It is only necessary to—"

"There's no sense in doing what has already been done," Leonardo interrupted impatiently.

"But it is enough for us."

Leonardo struggled to keep his equanimity. "I beg your indulgence, Father, but it's not enough for me. Once I have had a new vision of the Magi, the Virgin, and the infant Jesus, then I will take up the brush."

"Why must you be so difficult?" the cleric wanted to know.

"I never paint until I know I can impart some new truth in nature, or the heart, or the soul."

The monk couldn't think of a reply.

Not long after, Leonardo sat busily sketching in the sitting room of a brothel. All around him, prostitutes lounged on the richly upholstered furniture, or sat, flirting, on the laps of their customers. In one corner, a fat wool merchant happily accepted the caresses of a girl who had not yet left her teenage years.

Leonardo looked dispassionately at the scene. He was at work too. On his paper were the faces of prostitutes and their clients. One woman whispered to another, "What does he want here?"

The other replied, "Our faces, for his paintings."

Back in his studio, Leonardo's cartoon for *The Adoration of the Magi* was complete. It lay on the floor, where Paolo had pricked the lines of Leonardo's drawing with a stylus. Leonardo helped him temporarily attach the cartoon to the board, after which Paolo took a soot-filled bag and pounded it against the paper. When he was done, they removed the cartoon from the board, revealing the full outline for the painting, where the soot had passed through the tiny holes.

With a creative fire in his eyes, Leonardo studied the outline for a while. He grabbed a brush and a small container of pigment and began to paint.

Three weeks passed quickly. The morning light filtered through windows in Leonardo's studio. His breath turned to frost in the frigid air. Oblivious to the cold, totally absorbed with his painting, he worked on a detail.

The foreground was full of awed faces of those who wondered what this birth might portend for the future. It was easy to imagine their thoughts: The Savior of the world had arrived, and Judgment Day wasn't far behind.

The background was a cross between a cavalry skirmish and the rape of the Sabine women, an incident from Roman mythology. Everywhere in the painting was the sense of an event that had profound consequences for the future of man.

Finishing the detail, an oblique view of a woman's stunned face, Leonardo stepped back and surveyed the entire painting. Along with portraying the Bible story on which it was based, he had filled it with two elements: the yearning for spiritual meaning and order, and the will to survive the turmoil of war in which Italy seemed permanently mired. The latest battle between two Italian city-states was an almost daily topic of conversation among Florentines, whether or not it involved Florence. Leonardo seldom took part in these talks, but when he did, he held to his pacifist ideals: He wouldn't kill a fly, let alone a man.

Although the *Adoration* was far from finished, Leonardo was satisfied. He had broken free of convention and created a unique vision. He was fully himself as a painter. And he had proclaimed his artistic integrity, something he would fight to maintain at all costs, even while making a living.

Paolo watched in admiration as Leonardo worked on another area of the painting. The assistant warmed his hands by rubbing them together. Both he and the maestro wore heavy winter coats. A small brazier, for heat, sat nearby, but without any fire in it. There was nothing left to burn.

∼

Leonardo scanned some faces in a sketchbook. He studied one at length before picking up a paint container, looking inside, and setting it down. "Paolo, more of the very dark brown, please."

"That's all there is, Maestro. The light brown is almost empty too." He handed Leonardo another container, and Leonardo peered into that one. "You don't exaggerate, my friend." He dipped his brush and continued to paint.

"I wish we could stop and eat something, but there's too little food left," Paolo said. "And it's freezing, and we're out of firewood."

Leonardo kept painting. "The consequences of having no money, I'm afraid."

Someone knocked on the door. "Has our luck changed?" Leonardo wondered aloud. The monk from the monastery entered.

"Perfect timing, Father!" Leonardo exclaimed.

The monk studied the painting for a few moments. "Quite beautiful, so far," he finally said. "But it is taking too long."

"Nevertheless, my intention has been achieved," Leonardo countered.

"But you must finish the painting to complete the contract," the monk insisted. He was just doing his job. The abbot had told him he would be washing floors if he didn't manage this artist well.

"Father, if you want it to be done faster, I need more funds. It's cold weather now. I need fuel for warmth, I have no wheat left, no wine, and I am short of pigment."

The monk was annoyed. Payments were not his affair. He looked again at the painting and pointed at a certain part in the center. "There is a youth with an upraised finger, between the horses. Another boy beside the tree is doing the same thing. What does that gesture mean?"

Somehow, Leonardo found his last ounce of tolerance. "What does it mean to you?" he asked.

"They point to heaven, naturally," said the monk.

"Maybe you're right," Leonardo said.

"You don't know?" Now the monk looked confused.

"Here is my philosophy, Father," Leonardo said. "Viewers are free to take what meanings they see. The truth cannot be forced upon them."

"And what is the truth, Signore Leonardo?"

"It is what *you* think it is," Leonardo said. "Otherwise, it would not be your truth."

("God help me," thought the monk, "I don't want to wash floors." He decided on a different tack.) "What a mysterious young man you are, Signore," he said. "Just as we were warned."

"I'm a simple man," Leonardo countered. "It is the ultimate truth that is mysterious. Those with easy answers are often the leaders of state who send men into battle for a truth they insist is real, but that exists only in their simple minds."

"War is an unfortunate consequence of civilization," the monk declared. "But above the fray, there is truth in God." ("There! I've got him!" thought the monk. But it was not to be.)

"And what is God?" Leonardo asked.

The monk fell back on a stock answer. "The Holy Trinity, of course." He crossed himself as if to punctuate his sentence.

Leonardo was silent.

("Finally," thought the monk, "I've shut him up.") "This is a pointless discussion," he said sternly. "The abbot grows impatient for the painting."

"Tell him not to worry," Leonardo said. "I hold the entire painting in my mind. Well, everything except that to which the two young men are pointing."

"And when will you decide upon that?"

"I don't know."

"But the answer is obvious!"

"I, too, must find my own truth," Leonardo said. "Something I can observe directly."

"Careful, Signore," the monk warned. "On this issue, you tread very close to heresy." With that, he turned on his heel and left.

A few moments passed before Leonardo, cold and hungry, could speak again. Had he just seen his future? Was the whole world against him? His only crime was painting what he felt to be true. "Heresy be damned," he thought. "Does no one care about the truth?"

He called to Paolo. "Which do you think is worse? Being excommunicated or unpaid for my work?" Paolo could only shake his head in dismay. "This is our only commission," Leonardo continued. "I have looked for others and found none."

Paolo could see that Leonardo was sinking into despair. "You must have faith, Maestro."

Leonardo started pacing back and forth. "When people look at one of my portraits of a man, why can they say they see trees and hills behind him? It's just paint! I have created an illusion they believe. And yet, they're blind to the fact that I'm trying to paint the soul."

He glared angrily at Paolo, who shrank at the intensity in his master's eyes. "Anyone can learn to paint things that are there. But to paint things that one merely *suspects* are there… that makes life interesting!" He paused. "Unfortunately, that also makes me mysterious."

Paolo finally got the nerve to speak. "There are many simpler men who cannot do what you do. Maybe this makes you mysterious to them."

"You make a good point, Paolo," Leonardo replied. "Perhaps, four hundred years from now, if any of my paintings are still around, those who see them will say to one other, 'This painter from Vinci was at least going in the right direction,' rather than, 'This painter from Vinci was mysterious.'"

Leonardo slumped, as if he had already seen his own death ending in a pauper's grave. "I'm going for a walk," he announced.

That alarmed Paolo. He had heard stories of what desperate, struggling artists sometimes did. "I'm going with you."

"No, I want to be alone."

"But it may rain soon! You could get wet and catch a fever."

Leonardo put on another coat and left. Paolo said a prayer.

Chapter Eight

PAINTING THE CLOCK

Walking the streets of Florence, Leonardo encountered many scenes of the human condition. A ragged family pushed a cart containing all their possessions. They had no horse. When a wheel hit a pothole and stuck, the family pushed hard but could not budge the cart. The father called out to passersby for help and was ignored. Leonardo and a burly workman gave the cart another shove, and the wheel came free. "*Molto grazie, Signori!*" the father called out. Leonardo moved on.

He was nearly knocked down by a prosperous but unhappy-looking man who rushed past him in the opposite direction. He heard an argument above him and looked up to see a couple screaming at each other on a second-floor balcony. He looked down as an old man limped by with a crutch.

The scenes all around brought tears to his eyes. It didn't matter that everyone he saw was oblivious to his problems, his frustrations, his sufferings, his dreams, his very existence. They had their own frustrations, sufferings, and dreams. He felt helpless in the face of such misery. "I'm trying to give them beauty and truth," he thought. "If they don't understand it, there's nothing left for me."

Leonardo came to the Ponte Vecchio, a bridge over the Arno, and walked onto it. A wagon just missed him as it rolled by. He barely noticed. Midway across the bridge, he stopped to watch the water flowing below. Rain began to fall. Passersby hunched their shoulders and tightened their coats.

A sob escaped Leonardo's lips. No one heard him, or if they did, no one stopped to ask what was wrong. Feeling truly alone, he spoke to the sky. "Drown me, why don't you? I've accomplished nothing and have nothing to lose!"

He wiped his tears with his coat sleeve and leaned his head on his hands that tightly clutched the railing.

Someone tugged at his coat and Leonardo lifted his head. A young girl stood beside him. She smiled and looked into his eyes, blinking in the rain. In her arms was a crudely made basket of flowers. She chose one and held it out to him.

Leonardo forced a smile and took the flower. He wiped away the last of his tears, dug for a small coin, and offered it to her. She refused it.

"Why won't you take the money?"

The girl pointed at him, then traced an imaginary tear from her eye down her cheek. Leonardo was touched. He knelt down on the bridge to study her face.

"What is your name, Signorina?" She made a sign to him that she couldn't talk. "I see. But can you understand me?" She nodded. "That's wonderful. And so are you." He thanked her for the flower.

Through signs, she asked him what he did in life.

"Me? I'm a wanderer, looking for the truth of the human soul. There is so much misery in the world, and I have no answers. I can only try to give people some beauty and some hope. Even though I have none of my own."

The girl shook her head to contradict him.

"What do you know?" He studied her innocent face. She pointed to herself, then to Leonardo, and put her hand on her heart.

Leonardo was curious. "Love?"

She nodded enthusiastically.

"But what are we, that we have this inside us?" He indicated his body. "Is there more to us than this?"

The girl nodded. Leonardo took her by the shoulders. "I wish you could talk. What wisdom you could give me!" She shivered, and he took off his coat and draped it around her. He took her hand and put the coin in her palm. She embraced him lovingly, but his joy was greater than hers.

At the San Donato monastery, the monk entered the abbot's office. He was worried about having to wash floors. The abbot looked up from his desk.

"Father Abbot, I regret this interruption, but I must speak to you about the painter Leonardo."

The abbot stared at him impassively. "What is it?"

"I visited his studio yesterday to look at the painting. It's beautiful, Father Abbot. I would even go so far as to say that it's a brilliant masterpiece, unlike anything we've seen before."

"Then what is the problem? Have him bring it here so I can have a look at it too."

"It is not yet finished. He needs money to finish it."

"That was not part of the contract, Carlo," the abbot said sternly. "He must live up to his agreement, including his payment of the dowry."

"Father Abbot, he has no money for food or wood. If he starves or freezes, the altarpiece will never be finished."

Two days passed. The last of the wheat, which Paolo had kept from the scavenging rats, was simmering in a small kettle on top of the stove in Leonardo's studio. When it was gone, there would be nothing left.

Paolo had insisted on staying no matter what, but Leonardo wouldn't let him freeze or go hungry. He knew his assistant could find work elsewhere, and he determined to beat him with a broom handle if necessary to make him leave.

Leonardo shivered, trying to paint while Paolo broke up a small wooden stool and stuffed the pieces into the stove.

Poverty had worn lines in Leonardo's face. "Why have you stayed with me, Paolo?" he wanted to know.

"Faith," Paolo said.

Leonardo walked to the stove and warmed his hands. "Thank you," he said, as hunger gnawed at his stomach. He returned to his work.

Someone knocked at the door. "Paolo, can you go see who it is? I'm too frozen."

Paolo opened the door to see the monk from the monastery, a horse, a cart, and a driver. The cart overflowed with bundled stacks of firewood, bushels of wheat, and jugs of wine. Carlo, the monk, climbed down from the wagon and put his hand on Paolo's shoulder. Paolo promptly burst into tears.

"Compose yourself, son," the monk admonished. "I have brought what you need."

Carlo entered the studio while Paolo unloaded the wagon. Leonardo looked up, then past him to the open door and the activity outside. Relief passed across his face.

Carlo pulled a small bag of coins from a pocket. "You have saved us!" Leonardo cried.

Carlo studied the painting, which was much changed since his last visit. "I think *you* have saved *us*," he said quietly. Leonardo raised an eyebrow. Carlo handed him the coins. "I bring a message from the abbot. With this money, you may purchase more pigments. But before you return to the altarpiece, you must paint the clock on the monastery clock tower."

"Paint the clock?" Leonardo was taken aback. What fresh insult was this?

"Those were the abbot's terms," Carlo said apologetically. "They are better than freezing or starving, don't you agree?"

Spring arrived, and the weather turned hot almost immediately. Near the top of the San Donato clock tower, Leonardo sat in a chair harness, suspended by a rope, resentfully applying yellow paint to a large section of the clock face. He had already completed a blue border along the edges.

When he finished painting the face, he lowered himself to the ground and left the chair harness hanging. "Never again," he told himself. "I will soon be in a position where I can dictate my own terms."

Verrocchio's studio was nearby, so he decided to pay his former master a visit. Soon the two were drinking wine together and eating figs Leonardo had bought on the way. He knew that Verrocchio loved figs.

"But why Milan?" Verrocchio asked.

"I'm not much needed in Florence, except for painting clocks," Leonardo said.

Verrocchio laughed. "You know that's not true."

"At any rate, I'm finished with struggling in this town," Leonardo declared. "The abbot of San Donato thought he could lord it over me because I was hungry and cold."

Verrocchio smiled. "He succeeded, didn't he?"

"Look, my friend," Leonardo said, "I have much I want to accomplish aside from painting. But the constant worries about money hamper my research, my explorations, and my experiments. Paolo was chopping up furniture to burn in the stove! How can I concentrate under such conditions?"

"What can I do to help?" asked Verrocchio.

"I need a patron."

"Is that all?"

Leonardo ignored the jest. "And Florence is run by the Medici, who pay me no attention. That's why Milan."

Verrocchio shrugged. "In that case, I wish you great success there. But whatever you might think, you will be missed in Florence."

A few days later, Verrocchio threw a going-away party for Leonardo in an empty villa on the Via Carrara overlooking the Arno. Several long tables were crammed with well-wishers who feasted and drank. Leonardo, sober as usual, was the center of attention as he regaled them with funny stories.

Verrocchio sat beside him, with Aristotele, Botticelli, and Perugino nearby. Paolo and assistants and students from Verrocchio's studio enjoyed themselves. Musicians entertained the group with songs from the countryside.

"I will miss this place, and these people," Leonardo thought. Regardless of his recent financial circumstances, Florence would always hold a special place in his heart. He looked gratefully at Verrocchio, who had just given a somewhat incoherent speech about his former apprentice.

Perugino broke the mood. "I'm curious, Leonardo," he said. "Do you still persist in this foolishness about the independence of the soul?"

"Leave him alone, Pietro!" Aristotele insisted. "This is a celebration!"

"It's all right, my friend," Leonardo said. He looked at Perugino impassively. "The real foolishness is taking a purely scientific approach to that which is beyond science."

"Are you answering yes to my question?"

Verrocchio interrupted. "Oh, boys, boys! This is getting much too serious." He poured more wine and asked the musicians to play a lively tune. "Something to drown out this tiresome conversation," he suggested. The musicians obliged.

Botticelli spoke louder to be heard above the music. "Leonardo, when will you understand that the soul belongs only to God? And that it is beyond our understanding or control?"

"I think the soul *can* be understood," Leonardo said.

"Then tell us what it is," Botticelli demanded.

"Someday I will."

Botticelli scoffed.

At the convent of San Donato, a novice monk lit candles at the altar. Above him rested Leonardo's painting. Carlo entered, thinking to say a few prayers before mealtime. He was stunned to see the painting mounted above the altar.

"Brother, what is that doing there?" he demanded. "It's not yet finished!"

"I don't know, Father!" the young monk replied.

When Carlo showed up at Leonardo's studio, it had been stripped bare. "You can see for yourself," the landlord said. "The painter has moved out." He was shocked to hear the words "Damn him!" come from the lips of a monk.

A week later, a wagon arrived at one of Milan's city gates. One man drove and another sat beside him. Behind them were piled someone's worldly goods. A guard examined the contents, looking for contraband or something he could pocket and sell. He saw only paintings, crates, rolled-up drawings, tools, and odd constructions in wood and metal. He ordered the wagon to turn around.

Leonardo pulled a lute from a sack and played a happy tune.

"What's your business in Milan?" another guard asked.

"To bring beauty and happiness to its citizens," Leonardo answered.

"A leech. Go back where you came from," the first guard said.

"Shut up," said the other. "I like his music." To Leonardo and the driver, he said, "You can pass."

As they entered the city, the driver wanted to know, "How did you do that?"

"Music speaks to the soul," Leonardo said, smiling. "It is the representation of invisible things."

"If it's invisible, why pay attention to it?"

"Because the invisible directs the visible."

"That's ridiculous," said the driver.

"It got us into the city," Leonardo answered. "I want to understand that invisible something. Then I can paint it."

After the wagon had been unloaded and the driver paid, Leonardo stood in the center of a cramped, dingy studio. Its only good feature was a skylight in the roof. Leonardo sat on an unopened crate, loneliness on his face.

"The city of Milan welcomes you, Leonardo. Bravo! Bravo!"

He ate some bread and cheese, curled up on a pile of blankets, and went to sleep.

Chapter Nine

MILAN

The next day, Leonardo locked the door to his studio and walked around the neighborhood with a sketchbook. He was in a good mood. His life lay before him like a steaming plate of food, and all he had to do was dig in. He whistled as he looked through the shop windows. People nodded as he passed.

When he came to a noisy inn, he walked inside. It was nicely furnished and filled with people engaged in animated conversations. He sat at an empty table and ordered a meal.

Two hours later, with a half-empty glass and a half-full bottle of wine before him, Leonardo sketched an old man several tables away. A young man at another table stood and approached him. He was in his thirties, balding and intense. He wanted to see what Leonardo was sketching.

"Pardon me, Signore, do you mind if I have a look?"

"Not at all, Signore," Leonardo replied. "May I ask your name?"

"I am Donato Bramante," the man said. "Please call me Donato."

"If you will call me Leonardo."

They laughed and agreed. Bramante studied the sketch.

"That's the best draftsmanship I have ever seen," he announced.

"You do me a great honor," Leonardo said.

Invited to join Bramante and his friends, Leonardo brought his sketchbook. They passed it around, turning the pages.

"Bravo!" one said.

"You're a master," said another. "Where did you come from? There is no one like you in Milan."

"And the town is full of merchants who have no interest in art," a third said.

Leonardo spoke. "I am from Florence." Several ahhhs of understanding followed. "But I like it here already," he said.

The rest of the table cheered him, except for the man who seemed displeased with the town. "Why, for God's sake?" he wanted to know. "Milan is nothing like Florence."

"True," Leonardo replied, "but in general, I was not well understood there. I already feel more comfortable here. I sense no jealousy from any of you. Only brotherhood.

"The artists in Florence are busy trying to impress each other with their latest commissions," he continued. "And their patrons care about art only if it impresses their neighbors. But that is not what painting is about. It is about finding and giving truth."

"With ideas like that, we welcome you to Milan, Leonardo!" Bramante exclaimed. "You are one of us, and I predict that you will be our best advocate." He paused. "Except for Sforza, of course."

"Who is Sforza?" Leonardo wanted to know.

"Ludovico Sforza, Regent of Milan," Bramante said. "Perhaps you will meet him one day."

Three years went by, during which Leonardo made no progress establishing himself as a painter. His research in other areas continued. He improved his Latin and his mathematical skills, and he learned enough about mechanics to devise complicated machines. He could hold his own in almost any philosophical conversation.

But the savings he had brought from Florence were gone. He had closed his studio when he could no longer afford the rent, and he was running out of time to find a way to survive as an artist.

One day, he visited Donato Bramante, with whom he had become fast friends. Bramante was an emerging architect whose genius was beginning to flower. His studio was large, well-lit, and populated with assistants working on paintings, sculptures, and architectural models. When Leonardo walked in, Bramante was teaching them how to make a model of a medium-sized palazzo.

"*Ciao*, Donato!"

Bramante was overjoyed. "Leonardo, my friend, forgive me! I have been so busy, we have not broken bread lately." He took Leonardo aside. "How are things? I realize it's been difficult getting known here."

Leonardo told Bramante about closing his studio, then added good news: He had just secured his first significant commission in Milan through the Predis brothers, a family of artists. He would stay with them while they worked together on an altarpiece for the Chapel of the Immaculate Conception in the church of San Francesco Maggiore. The commission had been granted to Leonardo, Ambrogio de Predis, and Evangelista de Predis by the Confraternity of the Immaculate Conception of the Blessed Virgin Mary.

A week later, Leonardo was working inside the chapel on an advanced, very detailed sketch for the altar's center panel while Ambrogio and Evangelista sketched outlines for paintings of angels on the panels at either side.

Leonardo stepped back to get a view of all three. "Very nice, gentlemen."

"It's a pleasure working with you," Ambrogio responded.

"We are honored, Maestro," Evangelista added.

"No one has called me Maestro since Florence," Leonardo laughed. "But we are all colleagues here. I wish to be no one's maestro."

A priest entered the chapel and approached. "I'm glad you have time for laughing and joking," he said. "You must be ahead of your deadline."

Leonardo answered. "Actually, we're behind."

"Well, then..." The priest gestured toward the sketches, and the brothers returned to work.

Leonardo watched the priest as he closely examined each sketch, beginning with Ambrogio's. "Lovely," he said about that one. "Just as we wished." He moved on to Leonardo's sketch and studied it for a longer time. "This is not according to the conventions," he said. "Not at all."

"I don't paint conventionally," Leonardo said. "I do what my mind's vision tells me to do."

"Then please, Ser Leonardo, insert in your vision the following: gold leaf, a halo over each figure, brocade, precious fabrics, and a prophet in the background. And where are the cherubs?"

"I will insert none of those," Leonardo responded. "But I will tell you what is in my vision. These are also things you requested. To accommodate your wishes, I have added more presence of the natural world, such as blue sky, a bit of mist, flowers, trees, and many plants. And I will be dressing the Madonna in clothing the wife of a carpenter could reasonably aspire to, if she saved, over time, a little of the household money. Good fabric, and a jeweled clasp for her cloak."

For a moment, the priest said nothing. Then: "Very well. I trust the finished painting will be as you say." With that, he left.

Leonardo sat glumly in a chair and looked at the brothers. "Is this what I have to look forward to in Milan?"

"You did beautifully, Leonardo," Ambrogio said. "Just hold your position."

"I'm tired of holding my position. I wish no conflict with my fellow men. But I fear I'm doomed to it."

Two months later, Leonardo and the Predis brothers sat in front of the painted panels.

"I think it might be finished," Leonardo offered. "What do you think?"

"Our opinion is not important, Maestro," Evangelista replied.

Leonardo shook his head.

"We joke with you, Leonardo, but you are a master," Ambrogio said.

"Are we intruding on the Maestro?" said the priest from behind them.

All three turned their heads to look. With the priest was Danilo Moretti, who bragged that he was a painter, though he didn't paint much. He mostly partied, concealing his arrogance beneath a thin veneer of social graces.

The priest continued, "We have invited Signore Moretti to evaluate the panels."

"It is a pleasure to meet you," Leonardo said. "Would you like some wine?"

"No, thank you." Moretti indicated the painting, "May I?"

"By all means," Leonardo replied.

Moretti studied each of the paintings in turn. He spent more time viewing Leonardo's work, then turned to the priest.

"They all show technical expertise, especially the center one," he declared. "That is yours, Ser Leonardo, am I right?"

Leonardo nodded.

"Such technical expertise," Moretti murmured. "Where did you study?"

"I have studied life, Ser Moretti," Leonardo said. "But I apprenticed with Verrocchio in Florence."

"Very good. But I must tell you, I search in vain for emotion in any of your figures."

"My aim is to suggest pure feeling, not shout it to the heavens," Leonardo explained. "This style allows viewers to participate in it. To find the painting's core value for themselves. Not just pure feeling, but a wordless knowledge. That is what makes painting superior to all the arts."

"With that approach, Ser Leonardo, your work may be misunderstood," Moretti admonished.

Leonardo was unfazed. "Perhaps," he said. "I would rather be misunderstood than foist shallow understandings on people."

"Ultimately, Ser Leonardo, what are you trying to do?" Moretti asked, making a final attempt at one-upping the painter.

Not caring at this point what Moretti would say, or how else he might attempt to prove his superiority, Leonardo said simply, "I am trying to make visible the invisible that is in everything and that is not definable in words."

With that, the conversation was over.

Chapter Ten

FOOTHOLD

One morning, Ambrogio de Predis answered an insistent knock at the door. He opened it to see an acolyte from the Chapel of the Immaculate Conception.

"Is Ser Leonardo here?" the acolyte gasped. He had clearly been running.

"Yes. Why?" Ambrogio wanted to know.

"He must come to the chapel at once!"

"Is something wrong with the painting?"

"Nothing is wrong. The duke is coming to look at Ser Leonardo's panel. You should all come right away!"

At the chapel, a crowd of artists, intellectuals, and hangers-on surrounded the triptych mounted on the altar. They spoke in hushed voices, staring only at Leonardo's center panel, on which he had painted the Virgin, the infant Jesus, John the Baptist, and an angel, all surrounded by tall, craggy rocks. Father Natale, the priest, watched from just inside the door, eavesdropping on the conversation.

"The panel is ethereal."

"Like the painter, apparently."

"I've never seen anything like it."

"I hear he came from Florence."

There came the sound of many booted feet. A small column of armed troops approached, led by an officer. He told his men to halt, then approached the door. He peered inside the chapel, saw the crowd, and ordered Natale to clear everyone out.

When the chapel was empty, a man Natale knew by sight and reputation appeared. Ludovico Sforza, duke of Milan, had striking features and an aquiline nose. Wearing chest armor, he strode immediately to Leonardo's painting and dropped to his knees. He studied it in silence before beckoning the priest. Natale rushed to his side.

"This is a better painting than any in Lombardy," the duke proclaimed. Natale smiled, wondering if the duke's enthusiasm might translate into a donation to the chapel. The roof of the nave needed fixing. "We are most gratified that the work pleases Your Excellency," the priest said.

"This is by the Master Leonardo, the Florentine?"

"Yes, Excellency. Talented, is he not?"

"Milan has found its painter." The duke walked out without another word.

Leonardo and the Predis brothers arrived too late to meet the duke at the chapel, but Sforza had seen what he came to see. Soon after, he began sending his servants to hire Leonardo for small commissions. Word spread quickly about the painting in the chapel. Leonardo felt he had finally gotten a foothold in Milan.

Sunlight bathed the walls and roofs of Sforza Castle and streamed into the sitting room of the duke's mistress, Cecilia Gallerani. She was young and beautiful and held a white ermine in her arms. Cecilia was posing for Leonardo, who had softened the light on her face by hanging fine gauze over the windows. His portrait of her was nearly done. He had perfectly captured her soft, brown eyes, glowing with an intelligence far beyond her sixteen years.

"Tell me, Signorina, what is it like living here?" he wanted to know.

She thought for a moment. "Sometimes, I have a lot of fun with the Duke. Other times, it is very boring."

"And what do you do when you are bored?"

"I sit for portraits with interesting painters."

Leonardo laughed.

The ermine twisted in her arms, and she petted it to calm it. "When can I see the painting?" she wanted to know.

"When it's finished."

"And when will that be?"

"When it's finished."

Cecilia laughed delightedly. She allowed only the duke and Leonardo to tease her. "You are impossible!"

"No, just improbable."

Her face grew serious. "Perhaps, in another life, I will be the lover of a handsome painter." Leonardo continued to work in silence.

"Ser Leonardo," she suddenly said, "you must come to my gathering tomorrow night!"

"Your gathering?"

"Once each month, I bring together some of the great minds of Milan to discuss philosophy and other disciplines. I would be honored to have you attend."

"Signorina Gallerani, I thank you for your most gracious invitation, but I would be out of place among the great minds of Milan. And I would rather do than talk."

"Ser Leonardo, you are truly an original."

"That's better than being a copy."

She laughed. "Well, if you change your mind…"

The following year, Leonardo sat alone in his second Milanese studio. It was a smaller, more cramped space, with no skylight, and sparsely furnished. The duke's favor, like a summer zephyr, had come and gone, and they had not yet met face-to-face. Drawings lay scattered on the floor, and books, some open, some closed, along with unfinished paintings and odd-looking contraptions of metal and wood. Leonardo was writing a letter to his father.

My Honored Father,

It has been some time since I have written to you, for which I am truly sorry. I hope my letter finds you healthy and happy.

When last I wrote, I had just completed my portrait of the duke's mistress, which was well-liked by him and his court. But he never gave me further work.

Thus, I have languished, almost as obscure in Milan as I was in Florence. Thankfully, my friends and I have not been touched by the Black Death, which has taken so many lives.

While I wait for the duke to open his purse, I study the classics of Greece and Rome, and books of modern philosophy, arts, and sciences. However, I have concluded that learning through observation serves me better. My observations have inspired me to fabricate, even with my scant resources, various scientific and mechanical instruments that I hope will further man's understanding and conquest of his natural environment.

There remains only one aspect of human experience that completely eludes me. What is the soul? Father, please pray that the Creator grants me the ability to reveal the true nature of man, just as I have described his visage in my art.

Your loving son,

Leonardo

The next afternoon, the sky was a dull gray. Even the birds were silent. Carrying bread and wine, Leonardo walked quickly down the middle of the street, holding a handkerchief over his nose and mouth and avoiding the ghastly rows of dead and dying plague victims on either side. The air was filled with cries of grief and suffering. Masked workmen loaded the dead onto carts to be hauled away and burned.

A plague doctor approached. Dressed in waxed canvas and leather, wearing a protective hood with glass-covered eyeholes, and carrying a stick he used to lift infected sheets and view victims' bodies, he looked almost as horrifying as those he was meant to cure. Leonardo gave him a wide berth as they passed.

Reaching his studio, he went inside and shut the door behind him, trying to forget what he had seen and heard. Death was everywhere. He leaned his head against the door. Tears fell from his eyes.

A week later, at midday, Leonardo was busy sketching when he heard shouting in the street. He hurried outside. People ran past in panic and stopped suddenly to look up at the sky. In the middle of the day, darkness was falling. Leonardo realized what he was seeing. He had read about the phenomenon. A solar eclipse!

He rushed back inside and found a small device. Lighting a candle and grabbing a sketchbook, he hurried back outside. A man yelled, "God has sent the Black Death to kill us for our sins, and now he blots out the sun to hide the dead and dying!" Ignoring him, Leonardo viewed the eclipse through his device, having also read of the danger to the eye of looking at it directly.

By then, everything was black as night. But Leonardo's candle illuminated his face in the darkness. He stopped to write something in his notebook. He put it down and closed one eye. With his other eye, he looked again at the eclipse through his device.

Somewhere to his right, a woman shrieked, "Help us, God!"

Leonardo offered what little comfort he could. "It's all right," he said. "This, too, shall pass."

Chapter Eleven

SFORZA

Approaching Sforza Castle in a carriage that had been sent for him, Leonardo noticed once again the imposing towers and fortified walls. This day was special. He would finally meet the duke.

After passing over a moat and through several checkpoints with stern-looking guards, he was instructed that Sforza was to be addressed as Your Excellency. Leonardo was ushered into a room richly furnished with tapestries, gold and silver objects, shields, spears, and Grecian busts on pedestals. As he waited, he reflected on the morning's unsuccessful attempts to fit a piece of wood into the mechanism of a model of a flying machine. He had planed it down to make it fit, but he worried that he might have weakened it structurally.

Meanwhile, an elderly man stood in Sforza's private office, waiting to be noticed. The duke sat at a magnificent desk, leafing through an ornately bound volume of drawings of the Lombardy countryside. The elderly man coughed softly.

"Hello, Marino," the duke said, not looking up from his book. "Anything interesting today?"

"Good morning, Excellency," Marino said. "If you recall, you wanted to meet that painter-engineer. He is here and ready to see you."

"The painter from Vinci? Oh, yes. The altarpiece I liked in the chapel at San Francesco Maggiore." Sforza smiled. "That blasted Natale! He keeps pestering me for money to patch up his nave." He turned another page in his book. "So? What about Leonardo?"

"He has invented a device he used to view the recent eclipse without harm to the eyes. We thought his talents might be useful to you."

"Then bring him to me."

Leonardo soon found himself in Sforza's office. The duke was paging through a book of poetry.

"Your Excellency," said the elderly man, "here is Leonardo da Vinci, the painter and inventor."

"Do you know the poems of Ovid?" Sforza asked Leonardo.

"Only a few," Leonardo answered.

"This is from one he wrote in exile," Sforza said. He read aloud from the Latin: "*Laete fere laetus cecini*."

Leonardo translated: "When I was happy, I sang of happy things."

Sforza read on: "*Cano tristia tristis*."

"Now that I am sad, I sing of sad things."

"*Conueniens operi tempus utrumque suo est*."

"Each time suits its own work."

Sforza smiled. "What could make more sense?"

"Indeed, Your Excellency. But then, who knows? He might have been exiled for singing sad things happily, or happy things sadly."

The two men laughed simultaneously and heartily. Leonardo had won the duke over in an instant with his learning and wit.

Sforza looked at Leonardo for a long moment. "There is only one man in all of Milan who could recite Ovid with me, gaze at a dying sun and not go blind, and give the breath of life to a painting of my darling Cecilia," he said. "That man is you. Welcome to Milan."

"Thank you, Your Excellency."

Sforza came around his desk and embraced Leonardo. Leonardo wanted to mention that he had already been in Milan some years, and the duke had long known of his work, but he thought better of it.

A servant poured wine, then disappeared. Leonardo and Sforza sat on couches opposite one another. Sforza considered the clarity of his wine, sniffed it, and said, "This is a very fine wine from Franzacurta. My scholars tell me that even Virgil praised its merits." He looked at Leonardo. "Are you comfortable?"

"Yes, very, Your Excellency. Thank you." Leonardo had work on his mind and wanted to get back to it, but he also savored this moment.

"I fear that you have found Milan not quite pleasing to your sensibilities," the duke said.

"Not at all, Your Excellency!" Leonardo protested. He wondered what this was leading up to.

"Your Florence has so many talented artists that the city fathers can lend them without even missing them, while we Milanese—what do we export?"

"Armies?" Leonardo ventured.

Sforza laughed. "Exactly! A considerable accomplishment, since they protect the region, and other regions—even Tuscany—from invasion by the French."

"That is true."

"We Milanese have not originated a single great artist among us," the duke continued. "Professors in Pavia teach mathematics, medicine, and law, so we have many good poets and musicians. But few painters of any real merit." He paused. "Those painters we have describe themselves as being 'of the Lombard style.' But they only imitate the painters of Venice, Tuscany, and Flanders. Even my court architect, Bramante, comes from Urbino. I believe you know him?"

"Yes, I'm honored to call him a friend."

"Especially in these times," Sforza said, "a leader must have eyes and ears far beyond the walls of his palace. You come with the highest recommendations. Bramante is one of our best painters, but I value him more for his skills as an architect. Signore Leonardo, I believe that you are the great master we have been waiting for."

This was far more than Leonardo had expected. "You do me a very great honor, Your Excellency," he said.

"If you can manage to remain in Milan for an extended period, I'll make you live up to it," Sforza said. "After all, the Florentines may want you back someday."

"Your Excellency, before I left Florence, I felt for some time the need for a change."

"Then that's settled," the duke said. "The granaries are full here and so is the treasury. Although thousands have died from the Black Death, the city thrives, and peace is in the land.

"Just as the ancient Athenians were supreme among the Greek city-states, I have made Lombardy supreme among the Italian states. Not even the pope's armies dare challenge me. It is, therefore, time for me to make Milan the Athens of the modern world. And you shall help me do it."

Chapter Twelve

GRAN CAVALLO

When Leonardo next visited Donato Bramante, his friend's studio was even busier than before. "Donnino!" Leonardo called out.

"Leonardo!" Bramante answered. They embraced.

"To what do I owe the pleasure?" Bramante wanted to know.

Leonardo smiled broadly. "I met with the duke!"

"And?"

"Another commission. My time has come."

Leonardo gave Bramante the details over lunch at a nearby tavern. Then he shared his deepest concern.

"I have come a long way from humble beginnings in Vinci as an illegitimate child denied a proper education," Leonardo said. "Now I'm learning all the fields of knowledge, far beyond the arts. But I worry that I may not achieve my real goal: to be fully understood. This is more important to me than anything."

"Then why split yourself between so many fields of knowledge?" Bramante wanted to know.

"Because the branches of learning depend on one another. At the center of all is man. And at the center of man is…the soul."

"And why is that your concern?" Bramante asked. "Men have plumbed that secret for thousands of years and learned nothing. Leave the soul to God."

Leonardo smiled slightly. "You sound like a friend I had in Florence," he said, thinking of Aristotele. "But that's my reason for living, Donnino. To learn and show others the way."

Bramante could only sigh.

Several weeks passed. Back in his reopened studio, Leonardo worked on a painting while Paolo, whom he had convinced to leave Florence, sawed a piece of wood. Bramante rushed through the front door.

"Leonardo!" he exclaimed. "I have important news!" He noticed Paolo and looked questioningly at his friend. Paolo excused himself and left on an errand.

"And what is your news?" Leonardo wanted to know.

"An hour ago, a friend at Sforza's court told me that a commission for the great bronze horse honoring the duke's father will finally move forward. The selection committee will soon begin accepting proposals."

A monumental horse sculpture, cast in bronze, would be a complex and costly undertaking. Not even the Greeks or the Romans had managed such a thing. Naturally, Leonardo was interested in the challenge. And he loved animals, especially horses. Could he render one in bronze?

Already well known to the duke's palace guards—he was *il pittore del duca*, the duke's painter—Leonardo paid a visit soon after to Sforza's stables. He brought his sketchbook and a handful of carrots. He soon noticed a magnificent stallion and approached it for a closer look. The horse whinnied loudly and tossed its mane. Leonardo saw a stable boy nearby. "Boy, tell me about this horse," he said.

"He is the duke's prize horse, known as the Sicilian. He is easily excited. Strangers should leave him alone." The boy walked on.

Leonardo looked at the Sicilian. "Are you easily excited?" His voice was soothing and calm. Man and horse considered each other. "You are the most beautiful animal I have ever seen," Leonardo said. The Sicilian drew closer and sniffed the air. Leonardo pulled a carrot out of his pocket.

"If I give this to you, will you allow me the honor of sketching you?"

The Sicilian snatched the carrot and crunched it loudly.

"Then you agree?" Leonardo asked.

The Sicilian stood quite still.

"I see you," Leonardo said. "And you see me. I can feel you looking into my soul." He opened his sketchbook and began to draw.

As his sketch progressed, Leonardo knew that the Sicilian would be the model for his monumental horse. Offering another carrot, he asked, "Tell me, Sicilian, what do you know that we do not?" When the horse said nothing, Leonardo went back to shading the muscles of a flank with a bit of charcoal.

That night, Leonardo told Bramante about the Sicilian. "I have never seen such strength and beauty in an animal," Leonardo said. "What a charming individual he is."

"Why do you call him an individual, as if he were a person?"

"Because he is an individual. He is a soul in the body of a horse."

Bramante stared at his friend, bewildered.

"I spoke to him, and I felt that he understood me. I was told he could be difficult with strangers, but he permitted me to stay nearby and sketch him. Getting to know him has opened a new world for me. If I receive the commission, the statue will show that."

Bramante shook his head. "Leonardo, do you want to be known as the artist who talks to horses?"

"Maybe animals can teach us something of the spirit, and help us to see what they see."

"Why concern yourself with things we're not meant to know?"

"We have the potential to know, and the right to know. If God gave us life, why would he want us to stay ignorant?"

Bramante rolled his eyes.

"You scoff at me now," Leonardo said, "but someday, I will write what the soul is, and paint what the soul is."

"It is hard for me to understand this about you," Bramante replied, "because I see it as a useless search."

"You don't have to understand, just accept it as a part of me."

"That I can try to do."

Leonardo's artistic life began to revolve around the horse. Workbenches were cleared, clay and plaster were stocked, and sketches and models were underway. The sketches depicted a larger-than-life horse on a pedestal. Soon, models in clay or plaster stood nearby, like sentries.

One day, Leonardo, Bramante, and Paolo stood together at the end of a workbench, contemplating a beautiful scale model. Bramante spoke first.

"It's quite lovely. I think you should submit the proposal now, before someone else gets the commission."

"I'm not fully satisfied with it," Leonardo replied.

"When you get the commission, you can improve it."

Leonardo looked thoughtful. "All right. I'll submit it, based on your optimism." He turned to Paolo. "And tonight, when most people are at home in their beds, we shall go to the Ospedale Maggiore."

"Paolo, are you ill?" Bramante asked. Paolo said nothing, but his face was grim.

Later that night, Leonardo stood at a table in the basement of the hospital built by the duke's father in the 1450s. He was dissecting a corpse. Normally, he would have brought drawing materials to record his anatomical studies, but this time he had other plans.

Paolo watched Leonardo cut into the head of a cadaver, then turned away, retching. He despised these nocturnal visits. He had almost gotten used to the sight of intestines or a leg muscle and its underlying bone, but this was too much.

"Maestro, what are you looking for?" he asked.

"I've found what I've needed for my paintings," Leonardo said. "Now I seek proof that the soul once resided in the body." He pulled away flaps of skin and skull and made an incision in the brain tissue. Paolo turned away.

As they walked home together, Paolo said, "I don't want to go back there anymore. Unless it is very necessary."

"Because it makes you ill?"

"That, and because I'm afraid of what the church will say if they find out."

"Who cares what the church says?" Leonardo retorted. "I'm doing nothing wrong. The bodies are dead already. But don't worry, Paolo. I won't force you to go."

As they neared the studio, they saw a young boy waiting near the door. Leonardo recognized him as Gian Giacomo Caprotti, the son of a man who worked at a vineyard Leonardo owned near Milan. He was ten years old. In a rush of words, the boy told him his father had sent him to Leonardo to find work. There were too many mouths to feed at home, and he couldn't go back. He had no food or money and nowhere to stay.

Leonardo took him in, fed him, and made him a bed in a corner. The next day, he hired him as an assistant. Before long, Leonardo gave the boy a new name: Salai, or "devil." He was a thief. He was also a good assistant, and eventually a decent painter. He stayed with Leonardo for twenty-five years.

Several years went by during which Leonardo perfected his art, completed numerous commissions from the duke and various nobles, and immersed himself in many disciplines, always seeking ultimate knowledge but never finding it. On a bright spring day, he met Bramante at Santa Maria presso San Celso, a church where Bramante had recently completed a mural behind the altar.

"Welcome!" Bramante greeted his friend. "Come quickly and look!" He led Leonard into the church and stopped in the nave.

At first, Leonardo was confused. The choir area seemed to extend far into the distance. "I didn't realize the choir was that long," he said. "Isn't there a street just beyond the wall?" Then the light dawned. "You fooled my eye, Donnino! Well done!"

"I wanted you to see it, should you ever want to use this technique in your work," Bramante said.

"I would never steal your idea," Leonardo said. "How did you do it?"

"With paint," Bramante said, then explained how he had created one of the first, if not *the* first, examples of trompe l'oeil.

"I'm sure your trick will be copied many times, by parasites," Leonardo said. "And now, I want to talk with you about the bronze horse. I am not desperate for money, and I have been busy with other commissions since then, but my proposal has been with the selection committee for years. They are still deciding, and I have been unable to find a clear vision of the piece that makes me happy. I have decided to give up on the project."

Bramante put his hand on his shoulder. "That is because you do not know the latest news. I spoke with someone close to the duke only yesterday. The committee will announce their choice shortly."

"How shortly?" Leonardo asked. "Six months from now?"

"Less, or he would not have mentioned it," Bramante replied.

"If they picked someone, why didn't he tell you that?"

"He will when he can, Leonardo. And you'll know sooner than the general announcement, I assure you."

Two weeks later, Leonardo was working in his studio in Milan. His third studio was three times the size of his earlier ones. Workbenches and easels held engineering projects, drawings, and paintings. Strewn about were sketches of faces, muscles of the human body, building designs, plans for a town, and odd multi-geared inventions that were mazes of cogwheels. At one of the workbenches, Paolo consulted a drawing, then bent a small piece of metal as he held it with pincers. Beside him was a half-constructed clock surrounded by drawings of a completed clock and an exploded drawing of its parts. At the other end of the room, Salai swept the floor.

Leonardo came over to look at the clock. "Good work," he said.

Paolo shrugged. "It's your design, Maestro." His voice dropped to a whisper. "But I must speak with you."

"Then speak," Leonardo said.

"Salai has stolen something again."

"What is it this time?"

"An expensive stylus. And I need it to scribe where we will cut the metal for the model of the lifting machine." Paolo paused. "He bought himself a new tunic."

Leonardo sighed. "Why does he do it? I give him clothes and spending money. I don't understand."

"Throw him out!" Paolo urged.

"I can't. He'll starve in the streets."

"Because he's not willing to work!"

Now Paolo sighed. He knew this conversation would go nowhere. While the master had exacting expectations of him, Paolo, he let Salai get away with anything. "Buy another stylus," Leonardo said, "and hide it this time." He turned to walk away as Paolo shook his head.

Noticing a group of clay animals in a corner, Leonardo asked Paolo, "What are these doing here?" Paolo didn't answer. "I thought I told you to throw them out."

"But, Maestro—"

"I don't want to see them again," Leonardo insisted. "That horse has been a waste of my time."

"It has not," Bramante said from behind them. He had entered the studio so silently, neither Leonardo nor Paolo had noticed.

"What do you mean?" Leonardo asked sharply.

"My contact at Castello Sforza is the duke himself. He told me today that you have been granted the commission."

"Is this really true?" Leonardo wondered aloud. "Then I must find my vision for it."

"And you will," said Bramante, smiling. "You're Leonardo, of Vinci."

Chapter Thirteen

CORTE VECCHIA

Dressed in fine clothes, Leonardo rushed around his studio in a panic. "Where's Salai? He's late!" He leafed through stacks of drawings.

Paolo watched him with his arms folded across his chest. "Please, Maestro, you must speak with him. I gave him twenty soldi to get more supplies. He denies receiving the money, and we have no supplies."

"Why do you bring this up now, when I'm late and can't think about it?"

"Because we need these things in the morning."

"Well, buy some more!"

"Maestro, Salai is thirteen years old. He is almost a man."

"He will not change his habits," Leonardo said. "We have sufficient architectural and engineering commissions, along with small paintings for the duke, that Salai's thievery doesn't matter to me."

"But, Maestro—"

"He is like a son to me," Leonardo said. "And he shows promise as a painter. Now, where is the drawing for the armed, self-propelled carriage? The duke will want to see it."

Salai walked in, late to work, another habit that annoyed Paolo.

"Get ready," Leonardo told the boy. "You're coming with me. Bring a stick of charcoal and some paper."

Salai grabbed charcoal from a bench and dropped it into his pocket.

"Isn't your pocket full already?" Paolo sneered.

"Paolo! Not now!" As Leonardo looked through still more drawings, he barked orders at Salai. "Write this down! I must ask Maestro Antonio how to install castle ramparts by night, and tell Pietro how they built the tower of Ferrara without loopholes. I must study Maestro Gianetto's crossbow, as I have an idea for an extremely large, powerful bow for the duke's army. And get some more mathematical books, as I need to understand the squaring of a triangle so that I may properly design the portico for the church."

Leonardo finished paging through a sheaf of drawings. He grumbled loudly and moved to another pile. "I must find a hydraulics expert to learn about dams and their costs," he mused, thinking aloud. "Wait—the stonemason Pagolino is also a skillful hydraulic engineer. I'll ask him." Then, suddenly, "Hah!" He triumphantly held up a drawing and handed it to Salai.

"Roll this up and bring it along," he said. "Now, where is the carriage? We'll be late!"

Salai sighed. "The driver has been waiting outside for the last half-hour."

Leonardo and Salai rode through Milan's streets. Three large structures were visible: the cathedral (Duomo), a palace, and, at a distance, the duke's castle. Salai was taking notes as fast as he could.

"I need that herbal powder, and an animal bone from Doctor Marliano," Leonardo was saying. "Maestro Francese has promised to reveal to me the dimensions of the sun. Which reminds me: Aristotle's treatise on the heavenly bodies has just been translated into Italian. Get me a copy. I would rather read that than slog my way through the Latin."

Salai had just caught up when Leonardo added, "And I must ask the Florentine merchant, Benedetto Portinari, how they run on the ice in Flanders. Do they have special shoes for it? And I forgot that other drawing for the duke!"

"Which one?" Salai asked.

"The device to raise and lower the curtains concealing his collection of gold and silver plate. He may ask me about it. No matter. It's ready to fabricate."

Leonardo was finally done. Salai wiped the sweat off his brow and looked out the carriage window.

They came to a stop in a piazza dominated by an old palazzo, the Corte Vecchia. Artists, nobles, and politicians crowded around Sforza, his entourage, and a large object covered by a cloth.

Leonardo's arrival quickly drew attention. People came up to shake his hand and congratulate him. Followed at the proper distance by Salai, Leonardo approached the duke.

"Your Excellency!" Leonardo exclaimed. "Thank you for coming."

"Did you think I would miss this?" the duke said, smiling. "Although, I confess, I snuck a look at your horse before the sun had even risen, when only my guards were here." He beamed at Leonardo. "You have done a marvelous job with the clay original.

When you cast this in bronze, it will make engineering history. It will be something Athens would have envied, and larger than anything made by the Athenians or even the Romans."

The duke paused. "You should be very proud, Leonardo. I will want to speak with you after the unveiling." Leonardo nodded, and Sforza turned away.

After the politicians finished their speeches, Leonardo was introduced to the crowd to applause and shouts of "Bravo, Leonardo!" Tears of gratitude filled his eyes. He brushed them away and spoke.

"My friends, I am greatly honored that you are all here. Thank you for coming. And especially I thank His Excellency, Ludovico Sforza, Duke of Milan." He looked out at the crowd and up at the sky. "I humbly and earnestly hope that my work inspires the great creations that lie within each of you. I wish for you your rightful elevation to your own spiritual heights."

Two clerics in the crowd glanced at each other and frowned. What was this sculptor talking about? Spiritual heights? Did he mean the ascent to heaven after death? The rest of the crowd knew their souls were not their own; they belonged to God and the church. Confused, some wondered, "Is this artist also a priest?"

More applause and cheers broke out as Leonardo stepped away from the dais. He and the duke took hold of the rope attached to the draping cloth and pulled together. The cloth fell away, revealing the magnificent creation underneath: a stylized but accurate rendition of the Sicilian. Awed silence was quickly followed by a thunderous cheer. The crowd was one voice, crying out in triumph. The people felt the horse was meant for them. They instantly made it their own.

Leonardo nodded at Sforza and several dignitaries. Donato Bramante slapped him on the back. "Leonardo, you have done it this time!" he said. "This is a triumph for all Italians. Congratulations, friend! This horse will make you famous throughout Europe."

"What is fame?" Leonardo asked. "The glorification of a single individual? We are all great, Donnino. Especially you."

"But some are greater than others," Bramante smiled.

Leonardo shrugged as Bramante turned to greet another dignitary. Sforza waved Leonardo over. "Come to my tent for refreshments," he said.

Leonardo followed the duke and his guards. Salai ran up and handed him the rolled-up drawing he had brought from the studio. More guards at the entrance to the duke's tent checked to see that the drawing did not conceal a weapon, then let him pass.

The inside of the tent was sumptuously furnished. A table at the center was spread with a selection of foods and wines. Sforza poured two glasses of wine and handed one to Leonardo. "For the great artist and engineer from Vinci!"

"Thank you, Your Excellency."

Sforza eyed the rolled-up drawing Leonardo held. "Is that the armed carriage?"

Leonardo nodded and unrolled it on a nearby table.

Studying it carefully, Sforza murmured, "Holy Mother of God!"

Leonardo's drawing depicted a primitive battle tank—a concept hundreds of years ahead of its time. It was circular, with wheels and guns projecting from all sides.

"The armored battle carriage is steerable by a driver," Leonardo explained. "It holds many guns and light cannons, and it is powered by eight men inside, who use foot pedals to turn a system of gears that drive the wheels."

Sforza was fascinated and impressed. "Leonardo, when you came to us from Florence, you were already a marvelous painter and sculptor. I have watched your engineering skills flourish in Milan." He tore his eyes away from the drawing and looked at Leonardo. "I am appointing you Ducal Engineer," Sforza said. "With your help, Milan will surpass Athens in peace—and in war."

"Your Excellency, I hope for the day when there will be no wars," Leonardo responded, his face serious.

Sforza chuckled. "War is a part of life, Leonardo. We must face it and always be prepared for those who would destroy us."

"That's not all that man is."

"What do you mean?"

The mood was shifting. Leonardo could tell that Sforza felt challenged. He kept his voice calm. "Man is not naturally disposed to fight," he said.

Again, Sforza chuckled. "You are a strange one, Leonardo. A genius who preaches peace, yet designs marvelous killing machines."

"I suppose, above all, I'm a practical man, Your Excellency."

"Yes. Much to my delight."

Sforza swallowed the rest of his wine and poured more for each of them. Changing the subject, Leonardo asked, "Tell me, Your Excellency, why did you pick this piazza to display the horse? It is dwarfed in this space."

Sforza smiled cryptically. "Because it's close to my palace, and also to your studio."

Leonardo looked confused. "But my studio is all the way on the other side of—"

"Not anymore," Sforza interrupted. "As of today, your studio is there." He pointed to the Palazzo Corte Vecchia. "The entire east wing of the Corte Vecchia is yours in which to create great works of art and engineering for Milan and all Lombardy."

Sforza enjoyed Leonardo's stunned silence as the artist took in the magnificence of the palace. It had been carefully maintained by the leaders of Milan for the past two hundred years, and it wore its age well.

Leonardo finally managed words. "The whole east wing?"

"There will be no wasted space," Sforza said. "I'll keep you busy."

Tears came to Leonardo's eyes. Surely this was a gift from heaven. Was he in heaven? "I'm sorry, Your Excellency," he said. "I am overcome."

The duke put his hand on Leonardo's shoulder. "As were we all, when you unveiled the horse. You know, it reminds me of the Sicilian, my favorite stallion. What a coincidence, is it not?"

Leonardo didn't dare answer. Sforza laughed. "Don't worry. The stable master told me of your many drawings. I would like your best ones." Leonardo sighed in relief.

"That took courage, my friend. The Sicilian doesn't make friends easily." Suddenly, Sforza was dead serious. "You didn't ride my horse, did you?"

"Ride the duke's favorite horse?" Leonardo exclaimed. "I like living too much!"

They laughed together, but Sforza's tone wasn't lost on Leonardo. He wasn't in heaven after all. He briefly wondered what the future might bring.

Chapter Fourteen

THE LAST SUPPER

Leonardo stood on the piazza near his new home and studio. People were still showing up to look for the horse. He watched in amusement as a half-dozen frustrated artists with sketchbooks wandered back and forth, and thought about the letter he was writing to his father.

My Honored Father,

Bramante's prediction that the horse would make me famous has come true. People arrive constantly to view the sculpture, not knowing that we have moved it indoors to be cast in bronze. They come every day, even from France and Germany. Writers have composed poems about it. I wish you would come to visit me and see it.

Thanks to the duke, I moved my studio to the Palazzo Corte Vecchia. I have many projects under way, but the duke has given me the challenge of a lifetime. He recently set me to painting a mural on an entire wall in the convent of Santa Maria della Grazie. It will depict the last supper of Jesus, when he announces that one of his disciples will betray him. To show the profundity of this moment, in all its many facets, has become my passion.

His backlog of projects loomed in his mind, and he turned to enter the building as workmen came and went through the wide doors. They were making renovations to accommodate Leonardo's many studios.

The maestro walked into a vast studio on the ground floor, for which the walls of eight rooms had been demolished. A dozen assistants and apprentices were hard at work. Paolo walked among them, supervising. Leonardo happily joined him and enthused over the many things being accomplished. Salai lounged in a corner, reading a book. After making a tour of the studio, Leonardo sat at his desk and continued his letter to his father.

Although I have reached a more comfortable position, the war elsewhere in Italy worries me. As you know, Charles the Eighth has invaded Naples, along with the duke's army. Allying himself with a hungry lion, my patron plays a dangerous game.

Later that day, in the refectory of the convent, Leonardo stood on a scaffold six feet off the floor, working on *The Last Supper*. Several long dining tables had been moved away from the wall to allow the work to proceed. As he painted, thoughts crowded his mind. "This may eclipse the great horse. But the money goes out as fast as it comes in. I have so many assistants now, and so many inventions to be fabricated. They all cost money in labor and materials. I need more money. Always more money!"

He stopped, climbed down a ladder to the floor, and stepped back to contemplate the painting. It was carefully planned and partially completed. Massimo, a new assistant in his twenties, watched him. So did one of the Dominican monks from the convent, and a little boy who sat on his haunches in a corner. A tray of food sat untouched on a table.

"Maestro," Massimo said politely, "you have not slept or eaten for three days."

"This is my food and my rest," Leonardo replied, gesturing toward the painting. "But I will return to the palace now. Things are progressing there as well."

"Signore Leonardo," said the monk, "this painting is amazing! It is a discourse on the emotions. How do you imagine such things?"

"I don't imagine them," Leonardo said. "I simply observe what is there. Truth is all around us, if we only look."

Leonardo rushed out of the room. As the boy got up to follow him, Massimo handed him a coin and said, "For the sake of God, make him eat something."

Out on the street, the boy trotted to keep up with Leonardo. "Maestro Leonardo! Massimo says you should eat something. He gave me a coin for food, since you never ate anything in the refectory."

Leonardo didn't look back. "Keep it. Buy something for yourself."

They rounded a corner toward the Corte Vecchia. Leonardo went through a door and the boy followed. Once inside, Leonardo quickly checked on the first-floor studio, then climbed the stairs to a similar space on the second floor.

The second-floor studio was also vast. A flying machine in progress was the center of attention. A half-dozen assistants were in the final stages of building two giant wings and a fuselage made of wooden struts.

"*Ciao*, gentlemen!" Leonardo called as he entered the room with the boy right behind him. "How is our bird today?"

"We are on schedule, Maestro."

"Good!"

Leonardo approached one of the wings and examined it. "My glue is holding?"

"Yes, it's even stronger than furniture glue."

"But we all smell of rotten eggs," an assistant added. The others laughed.

"How many of you think it will fly?" Leonardo asked.

Seven hands shot up.

"You are very good assistants," Leonardo said. More laughter.

Leonardo and the boy proceeded to the third-floor studio. The boy's eyes widened. Surrounded by scaffolding, the clay horse stood in the middle of the room. On loan from a local foundry, a molding and casting foreman directed assistants, who marked faint lines defining sections of the sculpture. He noticed Leonardo and immediately approached.

"*Perfecto*, Maestro! We're just finishing where we will make the cuts for the molds. I have worked in lost wax for twenty years, but I've never seen it done this way."

"No one ever attempted a casting this big," Leonardo said. Walking toward the sculpture, he examined the lines to be used for making the molds. "Good," he said approvingly. "Be sure to reassemble it immediately after making the molds. Otherwise, the pieces will warp."

"But—"

"The clay original must be on display until the bronze is finished. People come from all over Europe to see this. They should not have to wait until it is cast in bronze."

Leonardo's attention went to the horse's shoulder. He climbed the scaffolding to get a better view, then traced one of the mold lines with his finger. He ran his hand along the surface.

"This is a problem," he declared. He moved his hand to the right. "The cut should be here. Otherwise, the wax will lock up when it dries and be very difficult to remove without destroying the mold."

"We will fix it, Maestro," the foreman said. Leonardo nodded.

Satisfied that all was going well in the palace, Leonardo returned to the convent, with the boy trailing behind. Passing through a market, Leonardo noticed a bearded young man inspecting an orange. He stopped, pulled out his sketchbook, and rapidly drew the features of the man's face. Returning the sketchbook to his pocket, he walked on.

"What did you draw?" the boy wanted to know.

"His face. He's perfect for Saint Thomas in the mural."

"Which one is he?"

"The one who points straight up."

"What does he point at?"

"If I only knew! Maybe you'll tell me someday." He looked at the boy and smiled.

Back in the refectory, the boy watched as Leonardo climbed the scaffolding and got back to painting. Then the boy went over to Massimo, dug in his pocket for the coin, and held it out to him. "He didn't want anything to eat."

Massimo sighed. "Then keep the coin."

"That's what I told him," Leonardo said from above. "He's an honest young man."

~

The next day, Leonardo went to Sforza Castle to speak with the duke's retainer. He wanted to be paid for work he had done so far on a project there.

The retainer was annoyed. "Ser Leonardo, you have been contracted to redo these rooms for His Excellency's new wife, the Duchess Beatrice d'Este. We've given you her instructions for redecorating, and the work goes very well, but you must complete the contract."

"I have no complaints about either the contract or my tasks here," Leonardo said.

"Then what is the problem?" the retainer wanted to know.

"I've been working on this for a month and have not been paid a single soldo. When I'm paid, I'll proceed further." With that, Leonardo stormed out of the room.

Back in his studio, still steaming from his talk with the retainer, Leonardo sat at his desk, pulled out paper and pen, and began writing a letter. The nib of his pen suddenly snapped. "Damn you!" he exclaimed. He threw the pen in the corner, got another from a drawer, dipped it in an inkwell, and returned to writing.

Soon he was in a carriage on his way to the duke's palace. He went over in his mind the letter he had written.

Your Excellency,

Regarding the decoration of the Duchess's apartments, I regret that the need to provide for my sustenance obliges me to occupy myself with trifles. If Your Lordship thought I had money, Your Lordship was mistaken. I have had to feed six persons for fifty-six months. Yet I have received only fifty ducats from the Treasury for all the work done.

Leonardo waited in an anteroom as the retainer read his letter. "Careful, Signore Leonardo," the retainer said. "Because of your delays, the duke has already threatened to have Perugino finish the work."

"So be it. But I have wages to pay my assistants. I need to be paid."

The next day, Leonardo sat in a salon in the east wing of the Corte Vecchia, reading a book, with Paolo nearby. An assistant ushered in the duke's private messenger, who held a parcel.

"Ah, Ettore!" Leonardo exclaimed. "What do you bring from the duke today?"

"Nothing from the duke, Ser Leonardo. This is from Gualtieri, the duke's treasurer."

"I thank you," Leonardo said. Ettore bowed and left.

Leonardo shook the parcel and heard the jingle of coins. He took a knife, opened the parcel, and poured a pile of coins onto his desk.

"Look, Paolo! A gift from Il Signore di Soldi."

"Bravo!"

"One of the best lessons I learned in Florence was about donkeys," Leonardo continued.

"And what was that, Maestro?"

"The silent donkey starves. The braying donkey gets fed. Do you see, Paolo? He didn't hire Perugino after all."

"Yes, but will that be enough?"

"If it isn't, they'll pay more."

∼

Compared to Leonardo's usual haunts, the home of Gianfrancesco Sanseverino, the Count of Carazzo and the captain of the duke's army, was small, but its interiors were luxurious. Outside in the cold night, numerous drivers waited in fancy carriages, trying to keep warm. They could hear music and laughter from the ballroom inside, which had been transformed into a theater. Before a crowd of one hundred nobles and important Milanese officials, a musical theater performance was taking place on a lavish set.

Suddenly, an actor emerged from within a flaming crowd. The audience gasped. A woman screamed. The performance continued to wild applause.

Leonardo and Donato Bramante stood at the back of the room with Carazzo, a sophisticated man in his forties who was all smiles. "Your sets are a joy to behold, Signore Leonardo," the Count said admiringly. "Thanks to you, I will be the talk of Milan tomorrow." A woman beckoned and the Count took his leave.

"There's great joy in entertaining people, is there not?" Bramante asked his friend.

"I would rather enlighten them," Leonardo said. "But this work pays for salaries, as well as studio upkeep."

"Your so-called 'studio' is three floors of a palace," Bramante commented drily.

"And none of those floors offers entertainment."

Bramante gestured toward the stage. "But this is also art. See how beautiful your design is."

"True art serves to awaken man from his slumber," Leonardo stubbornly insisted. "Other things purporting to be art are mere fluff."

The audience laughed at an actor's line. A nobleman approached Bramante and whispered in his ear. Bramante's face was suddenly serious.

"What is it?" Leonardo wanted to know.

"Beatrice d'Este has died in childbirth," Bramante said, "In one blow, our patron the duke has lost his wife and his son, who was stillborn."

"The sins of the father," Leonardo murmured.

"How do you mean?"

"Donnino, you know as well as I that the bread we eat and the coins we bank come from the pillaged towns and farms of Normandy." He paused. "I finished her new apartments just a few months ago. She was only twenty-one."

"We should go to pay our respects to the duke," Bramante said.

"Leave him alone, Donnino. Besides, he's sure to find consolation in other embraces."

Months later, the prior of Santa Maria della Grazie and one of the monks stood before *The Last Supper*. The scaffolding was still in place, along with assorted equipment, but the grandeur and solemnity of the piece were evident.

"He's amazing," the prior said in awe. "A genius! And finished at last."

"All but the face of Judas, Your Grace," the monk replied.

The prior studied the mural painting more carefully. "Where is Leonardo?" he asked, with an edge to his voice.

"We're not sure, Your Grace. He hasn't been seen here for months."

"Then find him! Go to the Corte Vecchia!" He screwed up his face. "It's ridiculous. A duke gives a mere painter the entire wing of a palace when his father built only a hovel for us."

"Your Grace, I wouldn't call this a hovel. It's a very grand—"

"Never mind! Get my carriage. I'll go straight to the duke."

Before long, the prior was installed in an easy chair across from Sforza, who was contentedly eating grapes.

"Your Excellency, it has been a very long time, and the painter is still not finished," the prior complained. "He has yet to complete the face of Judas."

"Really?" Sforza asked, spitting out a seed. "Tell me more."

"His equipment is scattered about our refectory, and the scaffolding remains in place, obscuring the view. It's mystifying how a man so talented can be so careless about completing his work. He has not been seen at Santa Maria della Grazie for months!"

After the prior departed, Sforza dictated a letter to a scribe.

My Dear Signore Gualtieri,

I require you, as my treasurer, to put pressure on Leonardo the Florentine to finish the work he is doing in the refectory of Santa Maria della Grazie, so that he can start work on the other wall in that room.

If he does not finish, all previous agreements concerning completion within a certain period of time will be canceled.

That evening, as Sforza signed documents at his desk, Leonardo stood before him. Leonardo was visibly angry, and the duke's former warmth and congeniality toward him were gone.

"I did not expect you so soon, Florentine," Sforza said.

"The name is Leonardo da Vinci, Your Excellency, and you have my apology for disturbing you this evening."

"Was it really necessary for you to come?" Sforza asked coldly. "My treasurer gave you his orders."

"I believe those orders came from you, Your Excellency."

Sforza gave Leonardo an oily smile. "As always, your insights puncture like a viper's tooth. But tell me, why should I pay you two thousand ducats a year, every year, to paint a mural you ignore for months at a time?"

"I work on the painting for two hours each day, without fail," Leonardo protested.

Sforza wondered for a moment if Leonardo was lying. But he knew that was not in the artist's character. He sighed. "All right, Maestro. But speed things up, will you? The prior grows impatient, as do I."

Another month went by. Leonardo's projects progressed as expected—all but the mural painting at Santa Maria della Grazie. The prior paid another visit to the duke and voiced his dissatisfaction. "We have yet to see Leonardo in the refectory," he protested.

Sforza wanted this business over and done with. He had tried to do a good thing for both the convent and Leonardo, and it had all turned to cow manure.

"As I said last month, he has only to paint the head of Judas to be finished," the prior went on. "He has come to see the mural just once in the past year. I hear that he spends much of his time working on a flying machine." He scoffed in disdain.

The duke's retainer appeared. "Your excellency, Ser Leonardo is here."

"Bring him in, and quickly," Sforza replied.

When Leonardo appeared, Sforza wasted no time. "What have you to say for yourself in the matter of the mural?" the duke wanted to know.

"With all respect to Your Excellency, and also to Your Grace," Leonardo said, nodding in the prior's direction, "there is no one at the convent who is schooled in art. A painter cannot labor like a workman with a shovel and a pile of dirt. While it is true that I have not been to see the painting for a number of months, I work on it for two hours every day."

The Prior was beside himself. "What?!" He looked despairingly at Sforza. "This discussion tries my patience to the limits. I beg to be excused."

Sforza nodded, and the prior took his leave with a final glare at Leonardo.

Sforza sighed. He tried never to annoy church officials. It wasn't good for his image. And should the matter of the mural drag on interminably, it might necessitate the purchase of more indulgences.

Although his father, Francesco I Sforza, had ordered the building of the church and the convent, it was he, Ludovico, who had made it the Sforza family burial site and rebuilt the cloister and the apse. His own wife, Beatrice d'Este, was buried there. Much had been invested toward achieving the goodwill of the convent, and it would be a shame to waste it. Still, he understood artists better than the prior did. Sforza indicated a chair, and Leonardo sat down.

"What shall I do with you?" Sforza asked.

"Your Excellency, I shall fall on my sword, as the saying goes, for the length of time the mural has taken to complete," Leonardo said. "But the problem has been Judas."

"He was Jesus's problem too, as I recall," the duke said, smiling only slightly.

"Judas was, as everyone knows, a malevolent and terrible villain," Leonardo went on. "His face in the mural must show his wickedness. That is why, for a year—morning and evening—I have visited the Borghetto, where all the ruffians of Milan congregate."

Sforza raised an eyebrow. Leonardo continued, "I have yet to discover the face I need. Once I find it, I will finish the painting in a day."

"I see," Sforza said. "But this cannot go on forever, Leonardo."

"Agreed. If my search remains fruitless, or your patience runs out, I will use the features of the prior for Judas, as he fits my requirements perfectly."

Silence hung in the room. Then Sforza gave up trying to keep a straight face and burst into laughter. "I fear you are right, Leonardo of Vinci! He does have the face of a demon."

Months passed. One morning, Leonardo was haunting the Borghetto, its usual mix of shady characters and impoverished shoppers sifting through second-rate goods at run-down market stands, when a man caught his attention. He wasn't merely ugly. He looked genuinely *evil*. Leonardo followed him at a discreet distance, noting every detail of his face.

That afternoon, Leonardo stood on the scaffolding before *The Last Supper*. He carefully painted in the face of Judas—the face he had seen in the Borghetto that morning. Paolo waited nearby, ready to assist. Behind him stood the prior, the monk, and several nuns, all watching silently. Leonardo put down his brush.

"Finally!" the prior exclaimed. He crossed himself. "May God forgive my unworthy thoughts about you, Ser Leonardo."

"And may he forgive mine about you, Your Grace," Leonardo said, climbing down from the scaffold. "It is done. Thank you for your patience."

"You have created a masterwork on our wall, Maestro. We are grateful to both you and the duke."

"It was my pleasure, Your Grace. We will clean up the mess and take out the scaffolding tomorrow."

Outside, with Paolo in tow, Leonardo remarked, "One foot in heaven, one foot in hell."

Chapter Fifteen

WHEN DREAMS END

As Leonardo and Paolo walked toward the Corte Vecchia, Leonardo remarked, "How marvelous it is that on the same day, we are ready to fly the machine and take the molds for the horse to the foundry!"

Paolo smiled, "*Si, certo*, Maestro! I only hope that Emilio is ready to fly." Emilio was the young man they had recruited—and paid—to take the first ride in Leonardo's invention.

Later that day, Leonardo and his crew carted the pieces of the flying machine up a windy hill overlooking Milan. Donato Bramante accompanied them. They assembled the device quickly, before the wind could weaken, and strapped Emilio's arms and chest to the wings. The moment of truth had arrived.

Emilio took a swig of wine for courage and sprinted downhill with the wind. For a brief moment, he was aloft. Then he crashed into the grassy hillside and rolled for twenty feet in a crackling maze of wood struts and fabric. Panicked, everyone rushed toward the crash site, where Emilio lay unmoving among the wreckage.

Before Leonardo, Bramante, and the others could reach him, Emilio regained consciousness and extricated himself. He looked a little banged up, but not too much the worse for wear. Cursing, he limped uphill toward the group, then passed them without speaking.

Leonardo called after him. "Emilio, are you all right?"

The young man didn't answer.

"Take heart, my friend!" Leonardo continued. "We will start over. Man will fly, and for longer than a moment. And you will still be the first!"

Emilio kept walking uphill. "You can all go to the Devil!" he yelled over his shoulder. "I'm through! I could have been killed!"

Leonardo and Bramante looked at each other and laughed, despite the gravity of the situation. Emilio was right. He could have been killed.

A mounted messenger appeared in the distance. The horse galloped toward them and was reined to a stop. The duke's messenger considered the wreckage at the bottom of the hill before saying, "Signore Leonardo, the duke requires your presence."

Later that day, Leonardo was ushered into Sforza's office. Sforza sat in a chair near his desk and gestured toward another for his guest. He looked unhappy and seemed reluctant to speak. Finally, he asked Leonardo, "Did it fly?"

"Very briefly, Your Excellency. But I have proven that man can fly, even if this was only a beginning."

"Well, good. But I heard that it crashed. Did the captain of your flying vessel survive?"

"Yes. He was angry but uninjured, except for a slight limp. I'll begin another machine immediately, once I determine a better design."

"And with a different captain, I'll wager," Sforza said. "I'm glad you're paying for it, not me."

Leonardo wondered why the duke had summoned him. "What do you require, Your Excellency?"

Sforza took a deep breath. "As you have no doubt heard, Louis the Twelfth has succeeded Charles the Eighth on the throne of France. I expect Louis to attack Italy, specifically Lombardy. I must prepare for war." He hesitated before continuing. "I have taken back all the bronze that was to be used for your horse. It is needed for cannons to fight the French."

Leonardo went pale. His heart pounded. Then his whole being erupted in protest. "But the molds are complete!" he said, rising to his feet. "They have been reassembled and the whole thing has been filled with wax! You can't do this! We're ready to pour!"

"I have already done it. I, too, had my heart set on that horse. It would have been a lasting monument to the founder of the Sforza dynasty and my legacy to Milan, and you would have made history with it."

Leonardo fell back into the chair. There was nothing more to be said.

Several days later, Leonardo and Paolo stood on the docks of the Naviglio Pavese canal, watching crates of bronze ingots being loaded onto barges. The first barge to be fully loaded slowly made its way south toward the foundries at the city's edge.

"I can't watch this," Leonardo said.

"Let's go, then," Paolo said. "We've been summoned by the prior of the convent."

"What now?" Leonardo wondered aloud. "Another petty correction to the mural?"

Later, in the refectory, Leonardo, Paolo, the prior, the monk, and several nuns stood before *The Last Supper*. The prior spoke first.

"Father Antonio tells me that you used an experimental paint mixture for our mural?"

"Yes, Your Grace. It was invented by Pliny in the first century, after the birth of Christ."

"I don't care who invented it. Just like your flying machine, your paint mixture has failed."

"What do you mean?"

"Look at the painting! It has only been a few months, and already the paint falls off the wall."

Leonardo and Paolo stepped up to the mural and immediately saw what the prior meant. Small bits of paint had curled slightly away from the wall. Leonardo touched one with a fingertip and it fell to the floor.

"Dear God!" Paolo exclaimed.

Leonardo was devastated. He looked down at the floor and saw countless flecks of paint. This time, his heart didn't pound. It felt as if a knife had been plunged through it. *The Last Supper* was ruined. Leonardo cursed himself for trusting a long-dead Roman.

The prior pointed a long, accusing finger at Leonardo and said, "I expect you to fix this immediately."

Leonardo turned to face him. "It can't be fixed, Your Grace." From where Leonardo stood in relation to the painting, it appeared that Jesus was sadly looking down on him. The prior glared at Leonardo for a long moment, turned, and left the hall. The monk and nuns followed.

Leonardo watched them forlornly. "Everything I touch falls away from me."

"That's not true," Paolo interjected.

"My bird, my horse, and now this." His voice rose to a cry. "I don't know what's important anymore!"

Paolo indicated one of the disciples above them—St. Thomas, standing to Christ's left, pointing upward with his forefinger. "That's important," he said.

Leonardo studied the saint, one of twelve he had painted on the convent wall. He sighed. "You're right." Then he put his arm around Paolo's shoulder and the two walked toward the door. "However, you have laid a fine trap for yourself."

"What do you mean, Maestro?"

Leonardo pointed upward with his forefinger, like the saint. "Now you have to explain to me what this means."

"It's beyond me, Maestro."

"It's beyond both of us, my friend." They smiled, somewhat ruefully, and kept walking.

In the summer of 1499, the French made further incursions into Italy and invaded Lombardy. Leonardo and Paolo stood on the roof the east wing of Palazzo Corte Vecchia, watching the activity in the street below. Evacuees of all ages were fleeing in carriages, on carts filled with their possessions, on horseback, or on foot.

Leonardo turned to Paolo. "Ally or not, it was only a question of time before the French turned on Sforza."

Paolo responded. "They'll be in Milan tomorrow. The duke has fled."

Leonardo sighed. "It's time to pack. Take only what is necessary. We'll have to leave the horse, the molds, and most of the drawings to their fate among the French."

Both men looked wistfully out at the city.

"It was wonderful while it lasted, no?" Leonardo asked.

Chapter Sixteen

CESARE BORGIA

By 1500, Leonardo had returned to Florence, the town of his beginnings as a painter. He was given lodgings and a workshop in a monastery in exchange for doing a painting for the high altar. His room and studio were humble but sufficient for his work.

One morning, he sat at a desk and wrote a letter to his friend Donato Bramante. Behind him was a very detailed, almost complete charcoal-and-chalk drawing of the Virgin Mary holding the infant Jesus, who was blessing another child. Mary was seated on the lap of an older woman, who looked at her lovingly and pointed heavenward with her left forefinger.

My dearest friend Donnino,

I long to share another feast with you in which we celebrate our successes.

Since the fall of Milan, I have wandered the peninsula for almost a year, obtaining small commissions in Mantua and Venice. But I have returned to Florence, as a guest of the Servite monks at the Basilica of the Most Holy Annunciation on the Via della Colonna. Do you know it?

They have engaged me to paint the Virgin and Child with Saint Anne and Saint John the Baptist, for which I am very grateful. Especially since the famous Florentine, Filippino Lippi, had been already selected for the commission. When he heard I was interested in it, he graciously bowed out, leaving it to me.

At around the same time, in the ducal palace of Mantua, where Leonardo had briefly stayed in his post-Milan wanderings, Isabella d'Este, the sister of Sforza's late wife, Beatrice, also wrote a letter. Composed in lavish quarters befitting the Marchesa of Mantua, who served as regent during her husband's absences, it was more ornate and formal. Isabella was twenty-six, pretty, and diplomatic but willful.

Most Reverend Father Pietro da Novellara,

We are writing you to request your assistance. If Leonardo, the Florentine painter, is at present in Florence, we pray you to inform us about the life he is leading, that is, whether he has some work in progress, as we have been told, and, if so, of what kind, and whether he is likely to remain long in the city.

Not long after, the Carmelite vicar Pietro da Novellara read Isabella's letter in his modest Florentine chapel. He was in his fifties, red-faced, and rotund, like an Italian Friar Tuck, only more powerful. He heard Isabella's words in his mind as he read them.

Would you have the goodness to ask Leonardo, as if the request came from yourself, if it would be convenient for him to paint a picture for my apartment? If he agrees, we will leave to him the choice of date and subject. If he is reluctant, try at least to persuade him to paint us a little Madonna full of faith and sweetness, as it is in his nature to paint them.

Since leaving Milan, Leonardo had become engrossed in mathematical studies. His studio was a jumble of papers covered with calculations, geometrical shapes, and mathematical expressions. One day, when his head was full of numbers, Pietro da Novellara paid him a visit. The two went into the courtyard to sit beside a fountain and drink a glass of wine.

The vicar spoke of Isabella d'Este. "She will pay you quite well, Signore. She is the Marchesa of Mantua and quite rich."

"I did a sketch for her when I was in Mantua," Leonardo said. "But I don't live only for money. And not for art, nor faith."

"Then what do you live for?" Novellara asked, slightly taken aback.

"For knowledge," Leonardo answered. "If I can't anticipate learning new things from a commission, I find something else to do. That is why I delve into mathematics and the sciences. To learn and to *know*."

Some weeks later, Isabella d'Este read Novellara's response to her letter.

After speaking with Maestro Leonardo, I find that the painter is indeed at work on a painting for the Servite monks, of the Virgin and Child with Saint Anne. Other than that, he has grown weary of the paintbrush. Aside from a Madonna for Florimond Robertet in Milan (that cannot be refused, owing to Robertet's position as secretary to the French King Louis), Leonardo devotes much of his time to geometry and mathematics. He conducts experiments in these fields to find what he calls supreme certainty.

Isabelle angrily threw Novellara's letter on the floor. "Supreme certainty be damned!" she exclaimed.

A year went by, during which Leonardo scrounged a living through various commissions with politicians and noblemen. One night in 1502, he was having dinner with Bramante in a popular tavern. Bramante was enjoying his successful reemergence in Florence from the ashes of Sforza's reign in Milan. Fortunately, the architect's fame had preceded him, and he was doing well.

"How long will you stay in Florence, Leonardo?" Bramante asked his friend.

"Long enough to find a prince."

Bramante laughed. "You sound like an unwed eldest daughter! By the way, I heard some very strange news last month."

"And what was that?" Leonardo wanted to know.

"Did you really turn down Isabella d'Este's request for a painting?"

Leonardo shrugged. "There are days when I regret it."

"Well, never mind," Bramante said. "Florence is full of princes and princesses, and some will no doubt be your patrons." He looked past Leonardo's shoulder toward the entrance. "Here comes one now."

Leonardo turned to see a young man enter with a beautiful woman on his arm. They were accompanied by a bodyguard. The tavern keeper fawned over them and led them toward the best table. On the way, various people in the bar approached him to pay their respects.

"Who's he?" Leonardo wanted to know.

"Cesare Borgia," Bramante answered.

"Ah. I've heard things about him."

Handsome but melancholy and just twenty-seven years old, Cesare Borgia already controlled the regions of Tuscany and Romagna, had proclaimed himself a duke, and was on his way through Tuscany to conquer Bologna. His power derived from Pope Alexander VI, who provided sufficient funds to support his illegitimate son's military campaigns. This included hiring the best condottieri to lead his armies.

"His motto is 'Caesar or nothing,'" Bramante said.

"Then he is aptly named."

Leonardo studied Borgia discreetly. "He doesn't look that vicious."

"Don't be fooled. He has left countless dead bodies in his wake. One of them was his brother, I'm told. I'll introduce you, if you want. But be careful."

"You know him?" Leonardo asked.

"Not well." Bramante drained his wine glass. "I designed a palazzo for him in Imola, that's all."

Moments later, Bramante and Leonardo stood at Borgia's table while Bramante made the introductions. Borgia looked with interest at Leonardo.

"Ah. The painter and engineer. Your reputation precedes you. Why don't the two of you join us as my guests? Leonardo, I want to hear all about your weapons and fortification designs for a certain former Duke of Milan."

Borgia and Leonardo got on well together. He was interested in Leonardo's stories and laughed at his jokes.

"Your friend has a sense of humor," Borgia said to Bramante. To Leonardo, he said, "You and I are much the same."

"In what ways?" Leonardo asked.

"Like me, you push aside restrictions and conventions of modern society to achieve your goal."

Leonardo nodded.

Borgia continued, "Come to my Florence palace tomorrow. I shall appoint you Ducal Engineer immediately."

Both Leonardo and Bramante were surprised.

"I've acquired the funds to hire five very capable condottieri, who are helping my armies unify the Romagna region," Borgia explained. "Your military engineering genius will complement their skills."

"I'm honored by the appointment, Your Excellency. I accept."

As he had with Sforza, Leonardo felt a mix of excitement and ambivalence. He had found his prince. Now what?

In the ensuing months, Leonardo traveled constantly between various military outposts and fortifications, using free passage papers signed by Borgia himself. The papers also specified that Leonardo, as a sort of military engineering inspector general, be treated with the utmost respect and given whatever he needed in the way of men, supplies, and maintenance to complete his mission. Further, that his advice on enhancing fortifications be acted on promptly and without alteration.

Leonardo took on his new responsibilities with his usual professionalism. The nature of his work saved him from any ignominy concerning unfinished commissions. But it was not without frustrations. Leonardo was a pacifist who believed that peaceful solutions were more lasting and beneficial than war. This fed the ambivalence he felt as Borgia's engineer.

One day, Leonardo stood with an army captain and his junior officers on the battlements of a castle, sketching improvements. He indicated the battlements, then pointed to his sketch. "The joints of the battlements could stand reinforcement like this, Captain Orsatti. And, at the same time, provision should be made at the bottom of the crenels for Grecian fire spouts, for pouring fire on the enemy."

On another day, near another battlefield, Leonardo was in conference in a commander's tent. Present were the commander, three line officers, and two civilians. "During the night, build up that redoubt to an elevation two feet higher for your cannons," he instructed. "That will give them greater range. Then bring your spare cannons up almost to the crest, but out of sight of the opposing forces. In the morning, when the enemy least expects it, you'll be able to move the cannons to the crest of the redoubt without delay and fire at will. The greater range of cannon fire will take them completely by surprise."

The commander gave orders to his officers and looked admiringly at Leonardo. "Maestro, I'm glad you're a painter," he said. "Otherwise, you would be the next Caesar." Everyone laughed except Leonardo.

Two weeks later, on a bluff above a lush valley near Ferrara, Leonardo stood with a general and other officers as they viewed a bloody battle taking place below them. Anguished screams rose from the valley floor. Everyone looked satisfied with the proceedings except Leonardo. The enemy soldiers were vastly outnumbered and were being viciously slaughtered by Borgia's troops.

"General, they beg to surrender!" Leonardo cried. "Why not show them some mercy?"

When the general didn't respond, Leonardo pressed him. "This isn't war. This is inhuman!"

Finally, the general spoke. "This is Borgia's kind of war."

Afterward, Leonardo agonized in his tent. He studied a drawing of one of his weapon designs—a chariot with three giant scythes for cutting down soldiers on the battlefield. He covered his eyes with his hands to shut out the view. Then he opened them and swept the drawing off the table.

Later that night, he met Bramante at a local inn. His friend was doing some traveling in the Emilia-Romagna region. The two sipped grappa as the innkeeper cleared their plates.

"It's fortunate you were in the area while we're here," Leonardo said. "I must be going soon. The army is moving farther upriver, under cover of night, to surprise the enemy."

Bramante studied Leonardo's face. "You don't look happy."

"All of this fighting distracts me from more important work," Leonardo said, trying to deflect Bramante's concern. But this was Donnino, and he couldn't not be truthful. His voice took on a note of despair. "What's the point of creating military designs for defensive use when butchers like Borgia use them for havoc and destruction?"

Bramante remained silent. "There is no point," Leonardo continued, "except to feed his insatiable lust for power."

Leonardo ruminated for a few moments. "I'll see you in Florence soon," he finally said. "I have to use my bank to pay my assistants."

"Why?"

"Because Borgia hasn't paid me yet."

By the next morning, Borgia's army had decamped and moved upriver. As soon as he was able, Leonardo packed his few belongings and hired a carriage and driver. With Paolo and Salai, he journeyed south toward Tuscany.

Once, when the carriage driver cracked a whip, Leonardo leaned out a window and hailed him. "Don't whip the horses!"

"I have to whip them to make them go fast," the driver protested.

"Then let them go slowly," Leonardo ordered.

"When do we return to the army?" Salai asked.

"We don't return," Leonardo said.

Both Salai and Paolo were confused. "Did you resign?" Paolo asked.

"No," Leonardo said. "I just won't return."

Chapter Seventeen

MONA LISA

Leonardo and Donato Bramante were in the garden of Bramante's villa on the Via della Scala in Florence. The setting had trees, flowers, and a broad lawn bordered with topiary in the French style. The two friends enjoyed fruit, cheese, and wine at a table on the sunny terrace.

"I'm through with war," Leonardo proclaimed. "It's madness. I'm staying in Florence."

"The right choice, my friend," Bramante agreed.

"Anyway, I've neglected a higher calling," Leonardo continued. "And I've already received a very valuable and prestigious commission that begins in October, as the building is being renovated."

"For Soderini, Gonfaloniere of the Signoria?"

"Yes. He rules our city fathers."

Bramante smiled. "Is it a painting?"

"No. A vast mural on a huge wall in the Hall of the Five Hundred."

"Then let us have more wine, in celebration," Bramante said.

The Palazzo della Signoria was the most impressive government building in Italy. Complete with a crenellated tower and battlements, it was originally built as a fortress palace and had seen many political upheavals in the two hundred years since its construction. It was an appropriate home for a mural created by Leonardo of Vinci for the Signoria, the ruling body of Florence.

The Signoria was dominated by Piero Soderini, a curmudgeon in his fifties. Having seen and admired *The Last Supper* in Milan, Soderini had entrusted the creation of a mural to Leonardo. The Hall of the Five Hundred was the largest, most important room in the building—in fact, it was the largest room in the known world—and Soderini had given Leonardo free rein.

One day in 1503, Leonardo and Bramante stood silently in the Hall, surveying the space. A huge cartoon, too big for any table, lay unrolled on the floor. In the drawing, which would be the mural's central tableau, opposing soldiers furiously struggled on horseback for a battle standard.

In a single image, Leonardo had captured all the brutality, insanity, and confusion of war, something he had seen firsthand as Borgia's armies laid waste to Lombardy and Romagna. His mural would be a thinly masked antiwar statement to Florence, Italy, and the world.

Bramante looked back and forth between the wall and the cartoon for *The Battle of Anghiari*.

"How ironic that you are called upon to paint this," Bramante said.

"War must cease," Leonardo answered, "or man will never be free."

"Or the reverse could be true. If man were free, war would cease."

"In any case, I shall move viewers, including our sainted city fathers, and educate them about the horrors that befall the sons they send into battle. As to the war with Pisa, I may be able to help end it."

"Oh? Well, good. It wastes our young men and drains our treasury. For this, the city fathers would be in your debt."

"They have paid it already, Donato. I received a commission to design a canal that will drain needed water away from Pisa. The city will be forced to surrender or die of thirst. Once peace is established and the canal reopened, it will provide a more stable supply of water for them and raise land values in the region."

Leonardo gestured toward the opposite wall. "Unfortunately, Michelangelo will create another painting there, the *Battle of Cascina.*"

Bramante was surprised by Leonardo's attitude. "You should be honored," he insisted. "Michelangelo is a fine painter."

"If only he could leave his abrasive manner at home," Leonardo said.

Bramante smiled, aware of Michelangelo's cantankerous reputation. He looked again at Leonardo's cartoon. "This is a bold conception, my friend. Your fame will rise to greater heights. Now be sure to finish the painting without delay."

Leonardo noted how the light from the windows fell on his wall. "That won't be possible," he said.

"Why not?" Bramante wanted to know.

"I have another commission."

Bramante raised an eyebrow.

"To celebrate his new home, as well as the birth of his second son, Francesco del Giocondo, a silk merchant, wants me to paint a portrait of his wife."

Later that week, Leonardo—by now in his second studio in Florence, which was larger and better appointed than the room in the monastery—was making a preliminary drawing of Lisa Gherardini, a woman in her twenties. She sat calmly and motionlessly, looking at the artist, fascinated by his good looks, intense eyes, and gentle manner.

Leonardo, in turn, was fascinated by her. Everything she did or said seemed imbued with an ethereal quality. What was it about her? The hours went by as he sketched. The question began to plague him. To complete her portrait, he would have to discover what made her special.

Using thin charcoal, he added a bit more definition to her eyes, then stopped to study her more intently.

"Am I an interesting subject to draw, Ser Leonardo?" she asked.

He smiled. "Very much so, Mona Lisa."

"And why is that?"

"I have seen things in the eyes of my subjects and learned much," Leonardo said. "But you are different. What is it about you?"

"I don't know what you mean, Maestro."

"I think you do."

In answer, she gave him a mysterious smile.

"That's it!" he exclaimed. "That's the smile for the painting!"

She laughed delightedly, then teased, "But now it's gone."

"Not at all," he answered, putting a finger to his head. "Your smile is in here now, and will soon be captured forever, so that you may mystify everyone else who sees it." He returned to drawing, then stopped again. "Damn! What is it about you?"

Leonardo's passion for the mural in the Hall of the Five Hundred was forgotten. He felt he was on the verge of finally knowing the secret of man. He drew on, barely able to contain his excitement.

"I must record your smile now, in case you never repeat it for me," he said.

"You mock me, Maestro."

"No! This is what I want—to show what is *underneath* life."

Lisa was speechless. She felt that the artist from Vinci had seen her truest self. He knew! And it would all be there in his painting. The one the fat, boring man she had been forced to marry would hang on his wall and show off at parties. She was lost, but Leonardo had found her.

She met Leonardo's piercing eyes. "Ser Leonardo, I beg you!" she exclaimed.

"I believe that you have lived before, and you know the secret of all secrets," he said, his voice cracking. "You know what the soul is!"

"To speak of such things invites excommunication," she pleaded. "You must stop!" She stood up, grabbed her cloak, and moved quickly to the door. She turned to look at him again. She had the sudden urge to run to him and tell him everything she knew and believed. Instead, she opened the door and walked out onto the street.

After a few moments of silence, Leonardo threw his charcoal stick against a wall, where it shattered into pieces.

Chapter Eighteen

SLINGS AND ARROWS

The next day, Leonardo was still profoundly disturbed by what had happened with Lisa Gherardini. He took a walk to clear his mind and sat on a large rock near a pond. Picking up a few smaller rocks, he idly threw them into the water, one by one. Then he noticed the ripples made by the rocks. A wave made by one rock intersected with the wave made by another. He noticed how each series of waves moved through the others without changing their nature or direction.

Back in his studio, he recorded his observation in a notebook, then announced to Salai, "I believe that still water, disturbed by a rock, does not move."

Salai looked at his master, wondering what would come next.

Leonardo continued, "The water only *seems* to move. Instead, it reacts like little wounds that open and close suddenly. It is more like trembling than movement across a distance."

Salai shrugged. He had long since grown used to Leonardo's musings. They were usually above his head.

Under Leonardo's patient tutelage, Salai had become a passable painter. Realizing that was all he would ever be, he took perverse pleasure in pilfering from the studio or spending money on trifles that should have gone to necessities.

Leonardo knew that Salai was even less of a thinker than a painter. Still, he kept talking in Salai's general direction. "Also, I sense that both sound and light travel through the air in the same way. But how does the eye see? What is the nature of light, beyond the possibility that it is made of waves?"

"Why do you ask questions that no one else bothers to ask?" Salai wondered aloud.

"Because I want to know everything, or everything I can know, so that I may one day gather and classify the whole of human knowledge, and then connect it," Leonardo proclaimed.

Salai laughed. "You can't do *that* in a day."

"But I have begun," Leonardo said simply. "And now I must do something that dismays me. I have no choice." He took a sheet of paper and began to write.

A sun shower was raining on Florence when the servant brought Lisa the letter from Leonardo. She was sitting near a window, knitting a shawl for her sick mother. She looked out at the garden before opening the letter.

My dear Lisa,

I regret to inform you that the demands of my large fresco for the Signoria, The Battle of Anghiari, *make it necessary to temporarily suspend my work on what will undoubtedly be a marvelous portrait of you.*

A tear ran down her cheek like rain on the window glass. The sky darkened, lightning flashed, and a thunderclap followed close behind. Lisa dried her eyes, left her knitting on an ottoman, and went upstairs to be alone.

She didn't believe Leonardo. Her portrait would not be finished. Even as she had dreaded another sitting, she already missed him and his pesterings about the soul. She would never be the same again.

In the Hall of the Five Hundred, Leonardo and Paolo stood on a scaffolding of Leonardo's invention. Connected to a series of gears and pulleys, it would move up and down or back and forth along the vast wall that had been prepared with a base for the mural. As Paolo turned a crank, he and Leonardo moved higher. Paolo loved his new toy.

"We have orders from other painters for these scaffolds," Paolo said.

"Let them wait," Leonardo replied. "We're too busy."

The scaffolding rose like the bellows of an accordion and stopped. Leonardo and Paolo attached the final section of the cartoon to the wall. It matched up perfectly with the section beside it.

Piero Soderini entered the hall. He was intense, tight-lipped, and slender. Leonardo greeted him. "Good morning, Gonfaloniere."

"Good day to you, Ser Leonardo." Soderini surveyed the cartoon, and Paolo began to pound a soot-filled bag over the pinpricks in the lines of the drawing.

"I see you have finished with the cartoon. Excellent!" He paused to take it in, then continued. "I have good news for you,

Leonardo. As one of the leading artists of Florence, you have been chosen, with other artists of your stature, to sit on a committee that will choose the site for Michelangelo's new statue of David."

Leonardo knew of the statue's magnificence. He had already seen it, but dreaded being in the same room with its boorish sculptor. Masking his displeasure, he said simply, "I'm honored, Signore."

A week later, Leonardo sat at a grand oak table in a meeting room at the Palazzo della Signoria. Wine, cheese, and fruit had been served. Around the table were many great artists of the day, including Pietro Perugino, Sandro Botticelli, and Michelangelo. Expressions ran from interested to apathetic, frustrated to angry. Shouts were heard from a crowd gathered outside.

Leonardo spoke, "I still maintain that such a fine statue should be inside the Loggia dei Lanzi, where it would not be harmed by sun, rain, snow, wind, or freezing temperatures."

Michelangelo protested loudly, "No!"

Everyone looked unwillingly at the ugly, unlikeable genius. Battered in his youth by a sadistic opponent in a fight, his nose was misshapen and his shoulders slouched. He walked with a noticeable limp.

"Why do you persist in this choice, Leonardo? My David should stand proudly in the blaze of the sun on the piazza, outside the palace!"

"And if storm and wind topple the statue and it breaks into pieces and marble dust?"

"It will be well anchored, you fool!"

More arguing ensued among the committee members. Michelangelo finally blurted, "Enough! You must choose! The crowd outside is divided in two violent camps about where to put my David. They throw stones at one another. Several men have already been injured! This is on your heads!"

Perugino suggested they vote.

After resolving that the *David* would stand in the piazza, the committee members left the palace and went their separate ways. Leonardo walked out alone, with Michelangelo not far behind.

They passed a group of young artists engaged in an animated conversation. One held a book.

"Look!" he exclaimed. "There's Leonardo of Vinci! He can explain it." He approached Leonardo and respectfully asked, "Signore Leonardo, do you have a moment?"

Leonardo paused and nodded.

"We are all admirers of your great works, Maestro," the young artist began, "but we have an unrelated question for you. We would love to know your opinion on a poem by Dante."

Michelangelo limped by, glaring at Leonardo. Leonardo gestured in his direction. "There's Michelangelo. Ask him." He turned to walk away.

The artists looked in awe at Michelangelo, who had overheard the conversation.

"Explain it yourself, Leonardo. You, who made a model of a horse you could never cast in bronze, then gave up, to your shame."

Leonardo stopped, speechless. How could someone be so talented and such a boor?

But Michelangelo wasn't finished. "And the stupid people of Milan had faith in you!" Leonardo knew that Michelangelo was referring to *The Last Supper*, which he had seen and rudely called "a child's drawing."

Refusing to trade insults, Leonardo walked on. The artists stared, stunned by what had just happened between the two creative giants.

That night, Leonardo wrote a letter to his father.

Dear Father,

I understand that you are visiting Vinci, our old home. I hope you are in good spirits, in contrast to myself.

The nib of his pen broke. He reached for a new one, installed it, and tested it on a scrap of paper before returning to his letter.

The loss of the bronze for the horse has become a curse that follows me wherever I go. It seems I am doomed to a life of triumph and tragedy.

Two weeks later, Donato Bramante knocked on the door of Leonardo's studio. When Leonardo opened it, he saw the somber look on his friend's face, and the letter he held in his hand.

"Is that my letter?" Leonardo asked.

He already knew the answer. His father had died.

The two men sat together for a long time, sometimes talking, sometimes in silence.

At one point, Leonardo sighed and said, "He helped me during my first years in Florence, but he rarely answered my letters. I learned not to expect a response. I suppose, being illegitimate, that I just wasn't important enough."

Some months later, during the rainy season, Leonardo was in the Palazzo della Signoria, working on *The Battle of Anghiari*. Outside, the sky was packed with dark, heavy clouds, and thunder boomed in the distance. Passersby on the piazza hurried to their destinations.

Leonardo stood on a scaffold, applying paint to a central section of the fresco where several horses and men converged in bloody combat. Paolo mixed colors. Salai dozed in a far corner. The high-ceilinged room was silent except for the sound of Paolo's stick as he mixed.

Church bells rang as a warning that rain was imminent. Paolo looked out a window at the piazza, now almost empty. Soon, rain began to fall in heavy sheets. Lightning flashed and thunder cracked simultaneously. The storm was directly above the palace.

Leonardo continued to paint. A drop of water hit his shoe, then another. He looked up at the ceiling. A dark line was forming where the ceiling met the fresco wall. Tiny rivulets began reaching down the wall.

"No!" Leonardo yelled.

Paolo turned to follow his gaze. "God in heaven!" he exclaimed.

"Light more braziers!" Leonardo commanded. "The heat will dry the paint and keep it from liquefying. Be quick, Paolo!"

Moments later, a row of braziers flickered below the fresco. Still, the colors were starting to run.

"It's the oil you used, Maestro," Paolo said, close to tears. "The heat is melting it! What will we do?"

"There is nothing to do," Leonardo said, grief and anguish written on his face. "The painting will be ruined. After the rains, they'll repair the roof. But it will be too late." He climbed down the scaffold and walked slowly toward the door.

"Maestro! You can't go out there. It's a flood!"

"And I can't stay here and watch the destruction."

Paolo grabbed Leonardo's overcoat and followed him. On the way out, he yelled at Salai, "Get up!"

"What?" Salai grumbled, rubbing his eyes. "Why did you wake me?"

"Pull the braziers away from the painting and extinguish them," Paolo ordered. "We're going back to the studio."

Outdoors, on the piazza, Paolo splashed through deep puddles as he ran to catch up with Leonardo. He threw the overcoat around his master's shoulders. Now in his fifties, Leonardo was twenty-five years older than he and subject to serious illness from exposure.

Paolo knew that Leonardo had put his heart and soul into *The Battle of Anghiari*, just as he had done with *The Last Supper*. Leonardo stopped to lean against a drenched wall.

"I could accept disappointments, if only I could learn a deeper truth from the endless searching," Leonardo said. "But no matter what happens, truth never comes." A sob escaped his lips. "It is always just beyond my sight. Always out of reach. Why?"

Paolo had no answer. As they moved on, they were as close as two brothers.

"I pray that you find what you seek, Maestro," Paolo said.

"And I thank God that you stand by me," Leonardo replied. "You always stand by me."

Chapter Nineteen

THE FRENCH GOVERNOR

Leonardo and Donato Bramante were dining at a table in a tavern garden. Leonardo looked glum. "I hoped, once the wall was dry, that I could repair the fresco and redo it with my existing cartoon. But each time, I met with failure. The paint mixture I need for this sort of work—and for that, I stupidly relied on Pliny—keeps melting."

"For God's sake, Leonardo, why don't you simply use the fresco technique?" Bramante exclaimed. "It has been working for hundreds of years!"

"I don't care if it was used in the Garden of Eden," Leonardo said stubbornly. "It doesn't allow me detail accuracy. Besides, I don't like the look of it."

Donato sighed.

Leonardo sipped some wine, then continued. "Donnino, to be honest with you, my heart is no longer in this mural. You know me. I pictured the painting in my mind. Once I did that, the excitement and challenge were over. Of course, to be paid, I went through the motions to fulfill the commission. But then…" Leonardo threw up his hands.

"Leonardo, your contract is for a real mural in the real world, not an idea in your mind."

"And for that," Leonardo said peevishly, "how have they paid me thus far? In coins of the smallest value they could find. As if I were a servant!"

In the Hall of the Five Hundred, the scene was reminiscent of the convent refectory and the piazza of the Corte Vecchia in Milan. Artists had come to Florence from across Europe to view and make copies of the *Anghiari* mural, just as they had flocked to Milan to see *The Last Supper* and the model for the horse statue.

Leonardo's painting was eighteen feet wide, seven feet high, and positioned roughly fifteen feet above the floor. Leonardo had, quite literally, risen to the demands of the space.

One artist commented as he painted, "It's a marvel! When will he complete it?"

Another, also painting, responded, "Never. He has abandoned it. The Signoria is very angry with him. Still, it adds so much prestige to the council chamber that that they won't remove it."

A third artist added, "They had better not remove it. Artists come from every workshop in Italy to study this painting."

"Ah, fate," said the first. "Three times, Leonardo has astounded Italy with a masterpiece, and three times he has met with catastrophe."

"Maybe he has a few more masterpieces in him."

"And hopefully, no more disasters."

On a chilly day in 1506, after a long struggle with the Signoria over the mural, during which he completed a few other commissions, Leonardo was reading a book in his studio when Paolo burst in and handed him a letter.

"Maestro! A messenger is waiting outside for your answer. It's from Count Charles d'Amboise, the French governor of Milan!"

"He is a powerful lieutenant of King Louis," Leonardo said. Reading the letter, he laughed out loud.

"Don't make the messenger wait outside in the cold," Leonardo told Paolo. "Bring him in and give him wine. And some bread and cheese."

The next day, in an office at the Signoria, Piero Soderini rose angrily from behind his desk and confronted Leonardo, who sat impassively in a well-upholstered chair.

"How dare you leave Florence when you have not finished the fresco?" Soderini demanded to know.

"I'm sorry, Gonfaloniere. It will never be finished—"

"Nonsense!" Soderini interrupted. "Just start over! Repaint it!"

"I've already gone over this with you—"

Soderini interrupted again. "You will abandon *my* painting for the French occupiers of Milan? It's a double insult to Florence!"

Soderini knew that he could not sway Leonardo. If the French wanted him to paint for them, the French would have him. Diplomatic relations were not worth spoiling over a spat about an artist.

Still, Soderini felt compelled to puff up his pride. "You have not heard the last in this matter, Leonardo," he warned.

"I would be very surprised if I had," Leonardo said.

"Be careful. Do not mock someone who can destroy your future as a painter."

Leonardo shrugged. "I have many futures."

At a loss for a response, Soderini grunted and motioned Leonardo out of his office.

Once again, it was time for a wagon trip to Milan. For Leonardo, this would be a victorious return. His days of obscurity were over. He would arrive as a celebrity and be treated as such. The country road on which he traveled with Paolo and Salai was dusty, but at least it was dry. The wagon was loaded down with the usual paintings and supplies.

As they rode, Leonardo sorted through letters and messages. He broke the seal on one and saw the scrawl of Soderini's chief scribe. For entertainment's sake, he read the letter aloud to Paolo and Salai.

> *His Honor, Ser Soderini, wishes you to know certain things on your departure from Florence. Since you are the unintended beneficiary of a tenuous state of peace between Florence and the Court of France, our allies in the war against Pisa, Ser Soderini graciously defers to Charles d'Amboise, the French governor of Milan, regarding your commitments to Florence. Ser Soderini has convinced the Signoria to grant you three months' leave from continued work on the Battle of Anghiari fresco. However, if you are late in returning to Florence, you must pay the city treasury a fine of one hundred and fifty florins.*

"Bah!" Leonardo spat, handing the letter to Paolo. "If Soderini didn't annoy me, he would simply amuse me."

Two weeks later, they reached Milan. The French flag waved inside Sforza's old castle compound. The guards spoke French.

Months passed, and Leonardo settled into his new position. One afternoon, Charles d'Amboise, a tall, humorless, sickly looking man of thirty-one, lounged comfortably on a couch, dictating a letter to a scribe. As King Louis XII's handpicked ruler in Milan, Amboise had taken over Sforza's old office in the castle.

Mon Cher Monsieur Soderini,

It is now more than three months since you so graciously allowed me to borrow Maestro Leonardo. However, he is far from finished with his commissions here.

Not only is he busy designing my new palace, he is creating portraits of some of the principal noblemen of my court. Therefore, I respectfully beg your leave to keep him in Milan, at least through the end of September.

To the scribe, Amboise said, "Sign it 'With high confidence in our long and fruitful Franco-Florentine amity.'"

A month later, Leonardo, dressed more richly than he had ever been in Florence, sat in Amboise's office, listening as the governor's retainer read Soderini's reply.

Ser Soderini understands the governor's position. However, Signore Leonardo received a large sum of money from the Signoria of Florence, but has only made a small beginning to the work he was commissioned to carry out. That work is meant to satisfy our ultimate supporters, the city of Florence. Therefore, we cannot release him from those obligations, nor do we wish his return to be further delayed.

"Et cetera, et cetera," Leonardo said, unimpressed. "A large sum of money? It was a pittance, and they paid me in one denari coins!"

"Mon Dieu!" the retainer exclaimed. "As if you were a beggar!"

"Please tell the governor that I like it very much in Milan. I spent eighteen years here, and now that I have returned, I have no wish to leave. I have many friends here and a number of commissions, including several for the governor. My design work for his palace in Porta Venezia is a long-term project all by itself."

He continued, "It's not right to abandon that to finish a painting in Florence that was cursed from the beginning and has brought me nothing but heartache. It may be that Gonfaloniere Soderini wishes to glorify war in his place of power. That would be an insult to God and to all the men who have died on the field of battle."

The retainer sighed. "War is the unfortunate consequence of the failure of diplomacy," he said. "We French have learned this the hard way."

"On that subject, we Italians are still in the schoolroom," Leonardo replied. "I accepted the battle painting commission because I thought I could show people how horrible war is for the men who must fight it. But it seems that an unseen power does not want a battle scene on that wall. Nor on Michelangelo's wall opposite. He left his commission unfinished and went to Rome to work for the pope."

The retainer raised an eyebrow at this. "Perhaps the Gonfaloniere thinks he can push you around because you aren't working for the pope? The governor will have something to say about that."

On a sunny day in Florence, eight members of the council sat around a table in the Palazzo della Signoria, discussing what to do about Leonardo da Vinci. All wore the crimson coats of their office. Four green-liveried servants stood respectfully nearby.

"The Frenchman Charles d'Amboise idolizes this painter," Soderini was saying. "Listen to this." He read aloud from a recent letter.

> *The excellent works accomplished in Milan by Master Leonardo da Vinci, your fellow citizen, have made all those who see them love their creator, even if they have never met him.*

Soderini put the letter down. "The governor would be much obliged if we were to increase Ser Leonardo's fortune, well-being, and the honors that are due to him who has given the invaders such deep inspiration."

One of the others spat, "Ridiculous!"

Another said, "Maybe Leonardo will inspire the French to leave Italy."

Soderini continued, "A messenger arrived yesterday from Amboise's vice chancellor, who demands that I stop pestering his painter. Even King Louis has joined Leonardo's chorus of defenders, having seen one of his Madonnas. And our ambassador to France has become enmeshed in these matters."

"Why are the French so concerned about a mere painter?" a council member asked.

"Because they have so few good ones themselves?" This was followed by hearty laughter.

"We now have an official diplomatic problem with a powerful ally, one that Florence cannot afford," Soderini said. "Need I remind you that they could always choose to turn on us?"

"Then what can we do?" someone asked.

"Per our contract with Leonardo, we shall immediately demand the fine of one hundred and fifty florins and be done with him!"

Someone added, "And we should whitewash his abomination of a painting!"

"No, no, no!" Soderini exclaimed. "We would be the laughingstock of all Europe! The painting is too popular. To paint over it would make us look like barbarians."

Not long after, Leonardo was forced to return to Florence to resolve a property dispute with his legitimate brothers. He took the opportunity to settle with the Signoria, easily paying their fine out of the abundant proceeds from his Milanese commissions.

One day, taking a break, he walked the hills above Florence with Donato Bramante. He fondly remembered the day he had crested a hill above the city with his father and seen the city for the first time.

"Was it wrong to wash my hands of the Gonfaloniere?" Leonardo wondered aloud.

"No," Bramante said. "Even unfinished, your *Anghiari* has been influencing a whole generation of painters. Raphael speaks of it with veneration."

Leonardo's attention was caught by a hawk spiraling overhead, riding the thermals. "Look, Donnino! Man will fly one day. It's only a question of when."

Several weeks later, back in Milan, Leonardo attended a garden party at the governor's palace. Nobles chatted at tables full of the best food and drink Lombardy had to offer. An ensemble played and sang a popular motet. Jester, jugglers, and magicians amused the guests.

On a raised platform with festive decorations sat Louis XII, King of France, surrounded by various relatives, advisors, and courtesans. Not far from the platform, Leonardo chatted with Amboise.

One of Louis's advisors leaned in toward the king. "Your Highness, I believe that tall man over there, the one speaking with Amboise, is Leonardo of Vinci."

Louis considered him for a moment. "He looks every inch the painter-philosopher-engineer. That is, if I dare presume how such a genius should look."

"If height is any measure of intelligence, Your Highness, no presumption is necessary." Louis smiled at his advisor's subtle jest.

Moments later, the advisor approached Leonardo and Amboise, said a few words, then led them both to the King. Leonardo bowed slightly. Amboise did the honors. "Your Majesty, please allow me to present Leonardo of Vinci."

Leonardo bowed again. "It is a very great pleasure to meet you, Your Highness."

Louis smiled. "It is possible that my pleasure surpasses yours, Monsieur. I have seen your work, and I count you among the greatest painters of our time."

"I am humbled," Leonardo replied.

"No need for modesty, Monsieur."

Amboise, who secretly wanted to keep Leonardo all to himself, continued. "As Your Highness is aware, Monsieur Léonard is equally brilliant as an inventor and engineer. His travels in the region on behalf of France have led to plans for pumping systems that will improve water supplies in the Lombardy region."

Louis nodded his approval.

"In fact," Amboise went on, "Monsieur Léonard is about to leave Milan again, briefly, to tour the river system in south Lombardy and design improvements in dams and other devices to be made along the Oglio, Ticino, and Adda rivers."

"Splendid!" Louis exclaimed. "We are happy that our esteemed friend is addressing the water needs of the region." He looked directly at Leonardo. "Indeed, Monsieur, I am sufficiently impressed with your accomplishments that I am appointing you Court Painter and Court Engineer, as of today."

Leonardo's face brightened. He had found a patron whose wealth and power surpassed even the Medicis.

Chapter Twenty

FRANCESCO MELZI

In the weeks that followed, Leonardo, Paolo, and Salai traveled through Lombardy on the engineering mission from Amboise. Everywhere they went, they were welcomed warmly by local French functionaries. One evening, after they spent the day surveying the Adda River, Leonardo's coach pulled into the courtyard of a country inn near the Vaprio d'Adda township. The three men went indoors for antipasti and wine.

Before long, an expensive-looking coach pulled into the courtyard. Out stepped Girolamo Melzi, a handsome count in the uniform of a Milanese militia captain. With him were his son and two attendants. Francesco, the boy, was fifteen, bright, and cheerful. Inside the tavern, the four claimed a table not far from Leonardo's and also ordered antipasti and wine.

Francesco stared in curiosity at Leonardo.

"That man seems very distinguished," he said to his father. "Do you know who he is?"

Girolamo sent an attendant to find out, who quickly returned and said a few words into his ear.

"He is the very great painter, Leonardo of Vinci," Girolamo told his son. "He has just been appointed painter and engineer to King Louis."

"Weren't you a painter before you were a soldier, Father?" Francesco asked.

"Yes, but I'm better at soldiering."

"Do you think Leonardo of Vinci would sit with us?"

Moments later, the innkeeper approached Leonardo as he was about to bite into a pepperoncino.

"Signore Leonardo, that officer"—indicating Girolamo—"has invited you to join him at his table, as his guest."

Leonardo glanced at Girolamo, who nodded cordially.

"Tell him I will gladly join him, as long as my assistants are invited as well. And don't forget to bring dinner out to our driver. I'll pay for that."

Soon Leonardo was the center of attention at the Melzi table. Francesco was fascinated by him.

"Signore Leonardo, my father has told me that you're a very great painter," the boy said.

"I wouldn't go that far," Leonardo said. "He is probably not acquainted with my work."

"Ah, but I am," Girolamo said. "My troops and I were stationed in Milan, not far from the convent of Santa Maria della Grazie. One of my lieutenants was aware of my interest in painting. Having been to the convent, he suggested I view your masterpiece of our Savior's Last Supper."

"I hope you forgave its state of degradation. A new paint mixture failed me."

"That didn't deter the line of people who had come from all over Italy to see it. As for myself, once I saw the work, I had the room cleared and a chair brought in so I might contemplate the painting alone, in complete silence."

Girolamo paused, remembering the experience, then continued. "I'm a simple soldier with no pretensions about art, and not much talent for it, either. I don't easily display my emotions, but your work so powerfully depicted the betrayal of Jesus, and his disciples' reactions, that I was overcome. I have never been so affected by a painting."

Leonardo was touched. "Thank you, Captain. That was the intended effect." Everyone laughed.

"Would you and your companions do me the honor of being my guests at my estate while you are touring the region?" Girolamo asked. When Leonardo agreed, Francesco nearly jumped for joy.

The Melzi estate in Vaprio was large and magnificent, befitting a Lombard count. Leonardo and Francesco sat at a table in one of the gardens, eating fruit. The villa was surrounded by gardens and orchards.

"I have been traveling for weeks in this region," Leonardo said. "Staying with your family in this beautiful villa is a welcome respite."

"My father could never afford all of this on a captain's salary," Francesco said. "He comes from a wealthy family."

"Money can be used for good or evil," Leonardo commented, plucking a grape from its stem.

"My father wants me to be a militia officer, like he is," Francesco said, "but I want to paint." Leonardo studied him.

In the banquet hall that night, Leonardo, Paolo, and Salai sat at a long table with Girolamo, Francesco, his two siblings, and Girolamo's wife, Alessandra. She was pretty, lively, and in her early thirties. The walls were decorated with tapestries and paintings of the Melzi lineage, along with their coat-of-arms.

A sumptuous meal was spread out before them. Girolamo raised his glass in a toast. "To our new friend, Ser Leonardo, who brings great pleasure and inspiration to the world through his art." The others raised their glasses and drank. Leonardo smiled and nodded to all of them.

Later that evening, in a large drawing room, Leonardo petted a pair of greyhounds that lay on the floor beside his chair. The Melzi family paged through a portfolio of his recent drawings.

"These are all of the Lombard countryside?" Girolamo wanted to know.

"Yes," Leonard replied. "If I see something I like, I stop the coach and draw it, for possible later use in a painting."

"I admire your balance of light and dark, Maestro."

"Thank you. It can help me bring truth to the viewer. Please allow me to offer one of those as a gift to you and your family for your hospitality."

The Melzis reacted with exclamations of appreciation.

Leonardo continued, "Now that you have seen my drawings, I would like to see Francesco's paintings. He has told me that he wants to be a painter."

This was followed by an awkward silence.

Girolamo spoke first. "That's very kind of you, Ser Leonardo, but I don't see how—"

"Francesco," Leonardo interrupted, "why don't you bring me some of your work?"

Francesco looked helplessly at his father. Leonardo saw what was happening. "If you would rather not," he said gently, "I will understand."

"Nonsense," Girolamo countered. "Francesco, get your paintings. I would like to hear Leonardo's views on your talent."

Leonardo understood Girolamo's meaning. Anything less than praise would put a stop to Francesco's ambition. But he would be nothing less than honest.

Before long, Leonardo surveyed several small paintings that leaned against a wall. Francesco looked nervously at the floor.

"Patrons of the arts should keep an eye on you, Francesco," Leonardo finally said. He meant it.

"*Molto grazie*, Ser Leonardo," Francesco said gratefully.

Leonardo addressed Girolamo. "Your son has quite a talent."

Girolamo was surprised by his own feelings. Naturally, he was proud of his son. He was also a bit jealous.

The next morning, Leonardo and Francesco walked together in the gardens. Leonardo stopped to sketch the view.

"Francesco, why do you want to be a painter?" he asked.

"To achieve the same visual perfection that nature possesses," the boy answered. "A perfection you have achieved in your drawings and in your *Last Supper*."

Leonardo laughed. "Did you think perfection was my goal?"

Francesco was confused.

Leonardo continued. "If you want to paint, you must keep this in mind. The painter who draws merely by practice and by eye, without any motivation beyond visual perfection, is like a mindless mirror that copies things without being conscious of their existence, let alone their deeper meanings."

Francesco pondered Leonardo's words. Sparrows chirped and rose into the air as the two approached a vine-shaded loggia.

"Look at the wisteria blossoms on the loggia," Leonardo said. "Is that not the most beautiful sight you have ever seen?" He glanced at Francesco. "You are a very earnest young man. I think you would be a good student and a loyal helper."

"If I ask to come and work with you, will you consider my request?"

"I will accept your request."

Francesco felt his life opening in front of him.

"And if you rise above your contemporaries by learning to look at nature with your mind and heart, not just your eyes, that will please me greatly," Leonardo added.

"Is that what is most important for a painter, Signore Leonardo?" Francesco wanted to know.

"I cannot speak for you, my friend. But I know what is most important for me. Not merely to paint, but to seek the ultimate truth. To find that truth and speak it through my work. Nothing is more important to me. Not love, not money or fame."

They walked beside a small stream. "Do you think it vain to believe I am worthy of discovering ultimate truth?" Leonardo wanted to know.

"No!" Francesco replied, surprised by the question.

"I ask because others have scoffed at me for having such a goal."

"I would never scoff at you, Maestro. Not for any reason."

Suddenly, Leonardo laughed. "What about my unfinished commissions?"

"Not even those. For you must have had good reasons to leave them unfinished."

"I am glad for your answer," Leonardo said. "Because I often don't finish commissions."

By now, they had been walking for a long time. Leonardo sat on a stone bench and rested. Francesco sat beside him. Leonardo breathed the fresh air, scented by nearby purple artichoke blossoms. He looked toward a distant stand of beech trees that screened the gardens and orchards from a neighboring estate.

"At times," he mused, "I feel I am cursed with monstrous losses. The bronze for the Sforza horse. The paint in my *Last Supper*. My battle fresco."

"And now you work for the French King Louis, like my father," Francesco said.

"I'd rather work for someone like Lorenzo de Medici. But he is long gone, like Florence's Golden Age."

Leonardo stood and went back to walking, with Francesco at his side. The Maestro stopped to look at a bee on a blossom.

"How do they know when the pollen is ready for them?" he wondered aloud. "Oh, God, life's mysteries elude me!" He turned to Francesco and smiled wryly. "Sometimes I think I'm cursed because I spend too much time on things that further my purpose but don't bring me any money."

"Curses are old wives' tales," Francesco said matter-of-factly.

"I see you have the cold scientist in you," Leonardo replied. "That's good. I think it will save us."

The next morning, Leonardo was in the kitchen of the Melzi villa, sketching the cooks at their tasks. They smiled shyly at him. No one had ever paid them so much attention. Francesco watched the drawing progress, and Leonardo taught as he drew.

"A representation of human figures should be done in such a way that the viewer may easily recognize the purpose in their minds," he said as he sketched.

"Yes," said Francesco. "I see."

"Good painting is technically very difficult. Even if you master that, and I think you can, you may never be understood as a painter. All of your work, even if it pleases you, may forever go unrecognized." He added a detail.

"I spent several years in Milan, in poverty, before getting consistent commissions," Leonardo went on. "I have seen very talented painters starve because they could not get enough work. And I have seen well-fed but mediocre painters who live in nice houses because they have the gifts of conversation and flattery."

"I don't care about any of that," Francesco said. "I just want to paint."

"But why?" Leonardo persisted. "To be a mirror?"

"I don't know what you want me to say!"

"If you have no purpose beyond painting pretty things, you should not be a painter. If you are not trying to uncover something deeper, something hidden, that is beyond what our eyes can see, what's the point? You're a Lombard count! You can live out your days in great comfort on this estate."

Francesco's face was a mixture of frustration and grief.

"I'm sorry, my boy," Leonardo said. "But if all you care about is taking commissions from aristocrats and oligarchs who fatten themselves on taxes levied on impoverished peasants, then—"

"Stop!" Francesco erupted. "I want more than that! I know that something is missing! No one can answer my questions! I thought no one else knew or cared about such things!"

The cooks had stopped their work to listen. Embarrassed, Francesco looked their way. They hurriedly went back to slicing meat and cheese and chopping vegetables.

Leonardo smiled. At last, he had found a student worth teaching, one who showed more curiosity than any of his fellow apprentices had, years earlier, in Verrocchio's studio. He had also found a comrade. Leonardo felt certain that at the end of his life, he could pass on his truths and his searches to Francesco. There was still much the boy didn't understand, but he was willing to learn. And he would come to know what was really important.

Tears came to Leonardo's eyes as he realized that all his life, up until this moment, he had been alone. Not even Lisa Gherardini, his Mona Lisa, had understood him as well, though she continued to prey on his mind in his solitary moments.

Later that day, Francesco went in search of his father. He found Girolamo in his study, working at his oaken desk. Francesco nervously entered and cleared his throat.

"What is it, son?" Girolamo asked.

Francesco approached. "Signore Leonardo…" He took a breath. "Signore Leonardo has accepted me to be an assistant in his studio."

"What?!"

"And I will study painting with him."

"This is an idle whim," Girolamo said sternly. "It is certainly no occupation for the son of a count of the Melzis, who will himself be a count one day." Girolamo tried not to think of his own failure as a painter. This was not about that, he told himself.

"Painting is the only thing I want, Father."

"And you think, at your age, you are old enough to know what you want?"

"Yes, Father, I do."

Francesco was surprised by his own courage. He was used to backing down in such moments with his father. But he had never wanted anything in his life as much as he wanted to study painting with Leonardo.

Girolamo loved his son, so he chose not to crush his hopes. He knew firsthand what that felt like. "I must think about it," he said.

"He's leaving in the morning."

"In my father's day, this would have meant a scandal. Disownment! Disinheritance! The estate would have passed to the next oldest son."

Francesco's expression remained as resolute as Donatello's *St. George*, which Girolamo had seen in Florence.

"I'll let you know my decision before he leaves," Girolamo said.

Francesco thanked him and left. That night, as he lay awake, unable to sleep, his father came into his room and sat on the edge of his bed.

"My son, venture forth in the world with all of our love and confidence in you. Make the Melzis proud."

The next morning, Francesco rode off in Leonardo's coach with the artist and his assistants. Girolamo, Alessandra, and their two younger children waved goodbye. His mother cried.

"Try not to be sad, Alessandra," Girolamo said. "He's a Melzi. He has spine and he has talent. He will acquit himself superbly in the field of life."

"But I will miss him so!"

"Take consolation that he's not riding off on a cavalry officer's stallion to a battlefield. He will be Count Melzi someday."

The family watched until the coach faded from sight in the hills.

Meanwhile, Francesco marveled at how Leonardo could study a book of mathematics on the bumpy road, and Salai watched Francesco with barely concealed jealousy.

"Ser Leonardo, why do you study so many different things?" Francesco wanted to know. Leonardo looked up, glad of the distraction. He had become a bit lost in Luca Pacioli's treatise. Even though he had collaborated with Pacioli and illustrated one of his books, he still found the subject matter daunting.

"Because knowledge gained in one area often leads to discoveries in another," he explained. "All subjects, and the study of heaven and earth, are connected."

Francesco saw further proof of Leonardo's thirst for knowledge not long after, in the basement morgue of Milan's Ospedale Maggiore, where he was made to watch Leonardo dissect the brain of a human corpse. Like Paolo before him, who had been relieved of such duties, he held a cloth over his mouth and nose. Looking at the boy's white face, Leonardo thought, "Why doesn't he puke and have done with it?" Instead, he said, "It's good to be back in Milan!"

"Signore Leonardo," the boy said through the cloth, "what are you looking for? This cannot possibly help your painting."

"What I seek is beyond painting." Leonardo pointed with the scalpel to a certain area of the brain. "All the nerves leading from the sense organs—the eyes, ears, nose, and tongue—terminate in this area of the brain. I see nothing that differentiates this area from any other area. Still, this must be where it resides."

"Where what resides?"

"The soul! I want to write what the soul is, in words or in paint."

"But that's impossible."

"So it has been believed for centuries," Leonardo said. "But I don't think anything is impossible. Some things are simply more difficult. If a man bends his will fully toward the task, anything can be accomplished."

He put down his scalpel and sighed in frustration. "It is said that all roads lead to Rome. I assumed that all nerves in the body would lead to the soul—right here." He indicated the brain. "But I was wrong. It's nowhere to be found. And even if I found it, how would I recognize it?"

Moments passed in silence before Leonardo spoke again.

"I have tried, in every way, to understand the soul. It seems to reside in the judgment, and the judgment would seem to reside in that part of the brain where all the senses meet. That part is called the Common Sense—the *senso comune*."

"This is beyond me, Ser Leonardo," Francesco admitted.

"The Common Sense is not all-pervading in the body," Leonardo continued. "As we can see from the different nerves leading to the sense organs, neither is it entirely in one part of the body. Unless something invisible is meeting them there. But what?" He threw up his hands. "As many intelligent philosophers, scientists, and physicians must have done before me, I have reached a dead end."

"Well, he's certainly dead," Francesco said, indicating the corpse.

Leonardo laughed. "Thank God for your sense of humor. But truly, it would have been enough for the eye to see on its surface, and not transmit the images to the Common Sense by means of the optic nerves. It would have been enough for the ear to hear, and the nose to smell. Instead, all those sensations are transmitted to the Common Sense. The soul uses the senses to perceive, but the soul itself cannot be perceived through the senses!"

"I am lost, Maestro."

"So am I! It's a puzzle of the highest order that no one has ever solved. And it was presumptuous of me to think that I could solve it. And yet, I must try."

Leonardo paced around the room. He felt he was on the verge of a breakthrough, and he was filled with excitement. "The Creator is divine," he murmured. "And just as we cannot perceive the Creator through the senses, we cannot perceive the soul." A lightning bolt hit his mind. "So the soul—the *human* soul—must also be divine!"

"Our soul?" Francesco asked. "My soul?"

"Yes!"

"Are you saying that we are all divine beings?"

"Yes!"

"That cannot be."

"It is! And we are!"

All the trappings of Francesco's young life—the wealth, the titles, the estate, the servants—fell away in a single moment, and he shouted, "Maestro, I understand!"

As they walked home from the morgue, Francesco felt that he and Leonardo shared a secret no one else even suspected. He knew why Leonardo had worked so hard to find it. Francesco wanted to tell everyone he knew, but he realized he would be scoffed at, as Leonardo had been.

This was revolutionary. It was counter to everything he had been taught, counter to the structure of society itself. "We are all independent spirits," Francesco thought to himself. "We are all divine!" He laughed out loud and skipped along the street ahead of Leonardo.

∼

One night, weeks later, Leonardo was working in his office at the studio when Paolo entered. Something about him was different.

"What is it, my friend?" Leonardo asked.

"I have found a young woman," Paolo said, "and we're in love. She wants to marry me and raise a family together."

Leonardo leaped up and hugged him. "I am so happy for you!" he exclaimed. "You have my most sincere congratulations."

"There's more," Paolo said. "I must settle down with her and cease my endless traveling."

"That saddens me, but of course you must," Leonardo said. "Should I find you a position in Milan or Florence?"

"We like Milan very much, and her family is here, so…"

"Then Milan it is. I will find you something right away. And we will still meet each other from time to time."

"That would be wonderful, Maestro. I'm grateful to you for that and much more."

"All I ask is for you to show Francesco what you do and how to do what he's not yet familiar with."

"Gladly, Maestro. Young as he is, Francesco's a hard worker. Unlike…"

"Salai? Yes, I know!"

Several weeks passed during which Paolo patiently taught an eager Francesco the finer points of working in Leonardo's studio. Not long after Paolo said his last farewells, Leonardo worked on the face of his still unfinished *Mona Lisa*. Francesco watched and sorted correspondence at the same time.

"Have you struggled much with her face?" Francesco wanted to know.

"Yes, but only because I'm trying to communicate something very difficult."

"What is it you are trying to communicate?"

"I came to this portrait with deep intuitions of my own that I have shared with you. I also developed an intuition about a smile that I noticed one day as we discussed something very personal."

"What did you see in her smile?"

"A wordless wisdom. The ultimate truth, or a hint of it. Something inexpressible. It may be just as inexpressible in a painting, and that is why I struggle. I wanted to know more, and I think she could have taught me."

"More about what?"

"The soul, and what is to come of us. As I told you at the hospital, the night I dissected the brain, I want to write what the soul is, in words or in paint. Ideally, both. That is the ultimate truth. I feel it, and I know Lisa feels it and knows more than I do, although she won't share what she knows. She refused to discuss it with me and left my studio in a great hurry. I never saw her again."

"Then what will you do?"

Leonardo was silent for some moments. "What can I do? I'm a painter. I'll paint John the Baptist, at least. He must have felt this knowledge. Perhaps I will learn more as I paint him.

"I see now that there is some mystical magic inside each one of us that we have completely forgotten. We are merely sleepwalking through life. I mean to wake us up."

Chapter Twenty-One

BETWEEN FLORENCE AND MILAN

The Palazzo Martelli in Florence was large and beautifully designed. One day in 1510, servants helped Leonardo, Francesco, and Salai unload baggage, supplies, paintings, and drawings from a coach and wagon parked in the carriage court. Leonardo replayed in his mind part of a letter he had written to Donato Bramante two weeks earlier.

> *A lessening of my work in Milan and an increase in commissions in Florence have forced me to split my time between the two cities. I have been invited to stay and work for some months at Palazzo Martelli on Via Zanetti. The Martellis are closely linked with the Medicis, and that bodes well for the future.*

A second coach pulled into the court, and Donato Bramante jumped out of the passenger compartment.

"Donnino!" Leonardo yelled in delight.

"*Ciao, bello!*" Bramante yelled back, running to embrace his friend. "My apologies! I only got your letter yesterday. Since you had spoken so much about me to Signore Martelli, he sent a messenger that you were arriving today."

"Well, here I am!"

"I don't have much time," Bramante said. "I must return to Milan tomorrow. Let's walk."

The two friends—two leading proponents of the Renaissance belief in the importance of the individual—set off into the streets of Florence. Man was emerging from hundreds of years of darkness imposed by feudal kings, princes, emperors, and the church. Leonardo and Bramante, painter and architect, held their lanterns high.

They rounded a corner and came face-to-face with Piero Soderini. The Gonfaloniere stopped in surprise, ignored Leonardo, and addressed Bramante.

"Congratulations on your latest commission, Signore. I look forward to seeing the finished building."

"Thank you, Signore," Bramante said politely.

"Unlike some Florentines, you actually *finish* your commissions," Soderini said. He nodded to Bramante and walked on.

Waiting until Soderini was out of hearing range, Bramante said, "What an ungrateful boor! He should get down on his knees and thank you for the *Anghiari*, which made his Hall of the Five Hundred famously fashionable."

Leonardo shrugged. "Pay him no mind."

"Artists from all over the peninsula now vie for space on the rest of Soderini's walls, just to be near your painting."

"Then I hope they fixed the roof." Both Bramante and Leonardo laughed at that.

"Speaking of roofs, Palazzo Martelli is a very fine temporary abode for you, but we should find you a good house in Milan that you can call your own, and maybe one in Florence too."

"There's no hurry, Donnino."

A month later, Leonardo was spending the evening in Piero Martelli's art-filled music room, listening to his host play the harpsichord and enjoying a glass of wine. Martelli was around fifty, friendly and intelligent, and Leonardo had indulged in many late-night conversations with him. He waited until Martelli finished playing before speaking.

"I am thoroughly enjoying my stay here, Signore Martelli, and I am very grateful for your hospitality."

"The pleasure is all ours, my friend," Martelli said, smiling.

"But I must soon return to Milan. My good friend Donato Bramante has found me a house in Porta Orientale in the parish of Santa Babilia, and I think I will buy it."

"A fashionable neighborhood," Martelli said approvingly. "You are relocating to Milan?"

"I will be back in Florence intermittently."

"You will be greatly missed when you are absent."

"That's kind of you to say. In truth, I haven't received as many commissions in Florence as I hoped. Certainly not enough to keep me in permanent residence."

Martelli looked genuinely surprised. "And why is that?"

"Florence may have soured on me because of the *Anghiari* mural."

"All of the painters in Florence idolize you!" Martelli protested.

"But they don't grant commissions. The Gonfaloniere does."

The next two years passed slowly for Leonardo in Milan. He had secured his house in Porta Orientale, but commissions were few and far between, and they barely supported him and his assistants. After yet another attempt to find more work, he arranged to meet with Amboise in Sforza's old office in the castle.

When he arrived, he was met by Amboise's retainer.

"I'm sorry, Ser Leonardo," he said. "The count has been called away unexpectedly."

"When can I see him?"

"Unfortunately, his schedule is very full these days."

An awkward pause followed. The retainer cleared his throat.

"I will tell you something," he said, avoiding Leonardo's eyes. "I can't speak for the other regions, but in Milan, as great as your paintings are, they have fallen out of fashion. Other painters have emerged to catch the fancy of the count and the people."

"I am a painter," Leonardo said. "What do you suggest I do?"

"Have you tried Florence?"

It was now 1512. Leonardo was sixty years old. He was frustrated, disenchanted, and worn down by age. He stood in front of an easel, finishing a self-portrait in red chalk. He had used strategically placed mirrors to view himself from different angles, and the drawing looked three-dimensional.

Francesco entered with a box of supplies.

"Where have you been, young man?" Leonardo asked sharply. "You have been away a long time."

"*Ciao*, Maestro! It took most of the day to get the special paper, pens, and charcoal you like."

Francesco took in the whole scene at once: the easel, the mirrors, Leonardo's dour expression. He knew that his lateness was not the cause of Leonardo's mood.

"May I see the self-portrait?" Francesco asked.

"It's nothing to show anyone," Leonardo said.

"Not even me? You have never denied me any of your works."

Francesco tried to come around the easel to view the drawing, but Leonardo blocked his path. Younger and quicker, Francesco got the better of him and stood in front of the drawing. Leonardo slumped in a chair nearby.

"This is amazing!" Francesco exclaimed. "It is as if you have composed a symphony with an image."

"My requiem," Leonardo said.

"Don't talk like that!"

"All right, I won't, in spite of how I feel. Tell me, what do you see in that face?"

"I see a man who is brilliant, persistent, and strong, despite his years."

Leonardo laughed bitterly. "I see a man who is tired, confused, disillusioned, irritated, and bitter."

"Maybe on the surface. But that's not the real Leonardo."

"No, you are right. The real Leonardo is a man who has failed miserably and is filled with nothing but regret for all he has left undone."

Tears came to Leonardo's eyes. Francesco pulled up a chair, sat near him, and listened.

"I have given up trying to use observable experience to understand the soul," Leonardo began. "I have gleaned nothing of value from philosophy texts nor from my anatomical studies, and I have perceived only vague hints of its existence from studying the subjects of my portraits. And even those could be my own imaginings."

He sighed. "I have wasted my life traveling down roads that lead nowhere. Maybe Mona Lisa was as much in the dark as I am, and she was too embarrassed to admit it."

Someone knocked on the street door.

"See who it is, Francesco. If it does not involve money, send them away."

Leonardo heard Francesco greet someone at the door, followed by the sound of footsteps. Bramante entered.

"*Ciao*, Maestro!" he said, smiling broadly. "What are you working on today?"

"You are the true maestro, my friend," Leonardo said. His voice was glum. "People live, work, and worship in your creations. Mine, they just hang on walls. Lately, they're not doing much of that."

"And that is why this is my first stop on my return from Rome. It is time to dispense with our endless journeys between Milan and Florence. I'm resettling in the city of the popes. There are more commissions to be had there. Important ones."

"I'm happy for you, my friend."

"Thank you, but I can't be happy unless I know you are also secure. Listen carefully to what I am about to say. I have learned something at the Vatican that you need to know."

Leonardo gave Bramante his full attention.

"The French rule over Lombardy is coming to an end," Bramante said. "Pope Julius has enlisted Swiss mercenaries to attack Milan. They will soon be at the gates of the city."

Francesco came closer to listen.

"I know that Amboise owes you much money," Bramante continued, "and that you have survived only through private commissions, many from the French. But they will be gone soon. Get Amboise to pay you before he leaves. And I urge you to come to Rome. I won't be able to help you when Milan is overrun with mercenaries, but I can get you work in Rome. I am well known to Cardinal Raffaele Riario, who is powerful in the Vatican."

Bramante finished speaking. Leonardo was deep in thought. Francesco waited to see what would happen next.

Leonardo finally spoke. "I expected the end of French rule and have been preparing to leave. But for you to make the trip here tells me again what a great friend you are, Donnino."

Donato nodded.

Leonardo continued. "Francesco's father has a fine estate in Vaprio and has invited me there to stay for as long as I wish. He wants to hire me to design plans for improvements to the villa."

"Excellent!"

"After I'm done there, it's quite possible that I will join you in Rome."

In March 1513, Leonardo was back at the Melzi estate, working in a makeshift studio that Count Girolamo had set up for him. He was designing a new wing for the villa. Francesco entered and brought him an envelope.

"A letter from Donato, Maestro! From Rome!"

"Ah. *Grazie!*"

Leonardo opened the letter and read it aloud for Francesco's benefit.

My dear friend,

I have much to report from Rome and elsewhere. The French were victorious at the Battle of Ravenna. Tragically, they sacked the city.

Leonardo paused, saddened by the news.

But, being much needed to defend France from the coming invasion of the Britons under Henry VIII, the French army has crossed the Alps and returned to their homeland. I pray to God that they stay there.

Leonardo looked relieved.

Pope Julius has died. He has been replaced by Leo X of the Medicis, who have also retaken power in Florence. Leo is quite a patron of the arts and sciences.

Two days later, at first light, Leonardo, Francesco, and Salai were in a coach bound for Rome. As they rode, Francesco read a book and Salai slept. Leonardo wrote a letter.

Dear Donnino,

I have finally taken your advice and am moving to Rome. Amboise paid me the funds he owed me, but I must stop first in Florence to put them in my bank. I look forward to seeing you and to loosening my belt with Roman cooking in my belly.

Your friend,

Leonardo

He folded the letter and handed it to Francesco. "Post this when we get to Modena, will you?" Francesco nodded. Leonardo smiled and looked out the window. The sun rose higher in the east, banishing the darkness.

Chapter Twenty-Two

FAREWELL TO A FRIEND

Leonardo kept his money at the Medici bank in Florence, an imposing, three-story stone structure in the middle of the business district. On a day in May 1513, he went there to deposit funds. Directed to wait at a desk in the main salon, he watched as a bank associate walked toward him, then brightened at the sight of someone behind him.

"Your Excellency! How are you?" the associate exclaimed. To Leonardo, he murmured, "*Momento, per favore.*"

Leonardo turned to see a well-dressed man in his mid-thirties who was accompanied by two bodyguards armed with swords and daggers.

The well-dressed man greeted the associate. "*Ciao*, Nicola!" Then he indicated Leonardo. "I see that you are occupied. Perhaps someone else—"

"The bank director will want to serve you personally," the associate interrupted. "I'll get Signora Costa for you." He hurried away.

"My apologies for interrupting your business here, Signore," the well-dressed man said to Leonardo.

"No matter," Leonardo smiled.

They sized each other up. The well-dressed man spoke first. "I have seen you somewhere before."

"And I you," Leonardo said. He stood and the two shook hands.

"I am Giuliano de' Medici."

"And I am Leonardo da Vinci. We met in the Court of Milan some time ago."

"Of course! How are you?"

"Very well, thank you. I have come to put money in your bank."

The two men laughed. Medici looked admiringly at Leonardo. "You are a very fine painter, as well as an engineer and philosopher."

"Thank you for the compliment. May I offer my congratulations to you on your recent assumption of rule in Florence."

Before long, the two were dining together in a private room at the Palazzo Medici, and Giuliano was asking, "You have no major commissions in Florence? I may rule here, but Rome is where you belong."

"I'm going there soon at the invitation of my dearest friend, Donato Bramante," Leonardo replied.

"Excellent. I know him also, and I like his architecture. Why not accompany me to Rome in my coach? I have business with my brother, Pope Leo. He has appointed me commander-in-chief of the papal armies. It will be a challenge to fulfill my responsibilities in Rome as well as Florence, but I shall do my best."

Medici continued, "Of course, we'll have you do commissions at my brother's court. And you'll have apartments at the Villa Belvedere in the Vatican."

Leonardo thanked Medici profusely. Commissions from the pope, and ensconced at the Vatican! Had his time finally come?

With its vast rooms for living and working, broad lawns, and lush gardens, the Villa Belvedere was everything Leonardo could have hoped for. Especially since Donato Bramante, the celebrity architect of Rome, chosen by the pope to design St. Peter's Basilica, was personally directing the renovations of Leonardo's apartments.

Francesco supervised several workmen who were moving boxes, paintings, and other possessions into a suite of rooms. Elsewhere, Leonardo watched as an artist applied gold leaf to ceiling molding.

"Excellent work, Giampaolo," Leonardo called up to him. "I see that our Donnino has given you precise instructions. But why isn't he here to greet us in person?"

Giampaolo climbed down from the ladder, his face serious.

"Ser Leonardo, I must tell you that Signore Bramante is very ill. The doctors say he does not have long to live."

Leonardo was stunned. "Why has no one told me this before? Take me to him immediately!"

Arriving at Bramante's large and beautiful house, Leonardo and Giampaolo were led up marble stairs toward the architect's room. Halfway up, Leonardo paused, holding tightly to the banister and trying not to break down.

"I need a moment," he told Giampaolo. "He cannot see my true feelings. He needs encouragement." Giampaolo waited patiently, understanding.

Inside Bramante's room, Leonardo nodded politely to the friends and family gathered there. Bramante looked shockingly small and frail.

"Donnino!" Leonardo exclaimed, wearing his biggest smile. "What are you doing? It's time to get better, get up, and jump back into life with me!"

"*Ti amo, amico*," Bramante said weakly. It broke Leonardo's heart.

Turning to face the others, Leonardo said, "May we have a few moments alone?" He waited until everyone left the room, then sat on the edge of Bramante's bed.

"We don't have much time left, my friend," Bramante said.

"Eh, such nonsense!" Leonardo protested. "You and I have many years to look forward to."

"God grant that to be true," Bramante said, coughing. "I will build you a great palazzo in Rome."

"You have already done that, Signore. Inside the Belvedere."

"Is everything to your liking there?"

"*Perfecto!* The apartments are superb, and it will give me great joy to live and work there."

"And how do you fare in Rome?"

"We have only just arrived, but already Medici has appointed me military engineer for the Papal armies."

Leonardo kept his face neutral, but Bramante knew what he meant.

"Don't worry, my friend. The Medici is no Borgia. He is interested only in defenses, in case the French choose to cross the Alps again."

"When will men realize they solve nothing by killing each other?" Leonardo said, shaking his head.

"Not in your lifetime, Leonardo. And certainly not in mine."

"Donnino, stop talking like that. You must get well so you can finish Saint Peter's."

Bramante reached for Leonardo's hand. "Whatever happens, know that I am deeply grateful for your friendship. We had some good times together, eh?" His eyes glistened.

Two weeks later, Leonardo and Giuliano de' Medici, along with a small contingent of Medici's personal guard, galloped on horseback across a bridge that led to a large fortress. Leonardo's long hair spread out grandly in the wind. Soon Leonardo, Medici, and Medici's adjutant stood on the battlements above the fortress gate, looking down at the terrain. The adjutant had writing materials at the ready.

Leonardo indicated the ground below them, not far from the fortress wall. "The first order of business is to dig a trench about six hundred braccia long." The adjutant took notes. Pointing, Leonardo continued, "The trench should go from there to there, and sharpened spokes should be placed upright along its length." He gestured toward a hill. "Next, flatten that and you'll achieve a more open line of fire against any attacking forces."

"Brilliant and costly," Medici commented. To his adjutant, he said, "See that it's done."

The adjutant nodded. "Yes, Your Excellency."

"I will calculate the number of workers, how many days it will take, and the cost in labor," Leonardo offered.

Medici laughed. "God smiled at me, Leonardo, when he had you do your banking with my family."

Leonardo turned toward the castle keep. "The central tower of the keep is high but defenseless at ground level." Medici and his adjutant listened attentively. "If you provide pyramidal structures, with devious entrances, at the corners, and then add ditches all the way around it, the keep will have great resistance to any opposing force, all by itself."

"Pope Leo has assigned me the task of draining the Pontine marshes southeast of Rome," Medici said, changing the subject.

Without skipping a beat, Leonardo replied, "I know the area from an earlier visit. I will draw up engineering and hydraulic plans, as well as designs for two canals that will furnish outlets for the Ufente River."

By early 1514, Leonardo was accustomed to life in the Vatican. One day, he watched as a prelate showed him the vellum pages of an ancient text spread out on a broad table.

"These calfskin parchments are a small part of my collection of tablets, papyrus scrolls, and such. According to our scholars, they date from the time our Lord preached in the Holy Land."

Leonardo was transfixed. "Fascinating material! I would appreciate the opportunity to study them at length."

"You're very welcome to do so, Leonardo." He sat heavily on a sofa and indicated a chair for Leonardo.

"My staff informed me that you wish to inquire about possible painting or sculpture commissions?"

"Yes, Your Grace."

"To be frank with you, His Holiness has deemed it appropriate to give the painter Raphael many more commissions than were previously envisioned. And in spite of all the fuss with Michelangelo over the Sistine Chapel ceiling, His Holiness is pleased with it and has told me that he favors Michelangelo for the large sculpture commission for the tomb of his predecessor, Pope Julius."

Leonardo was impassive. "I see."

The prelate continued. "Regrettably, the important commissions have already been assigned. This trend is likely to continue."

Leonardo stiffened in his chair. Clearly, this cleric was not going to help him.

"However," the prelate went on, "your reputation is well known to the Medicis, and you can rest in the certain knowledge that your highly respected past body of work will live on."

"My reputation doesn't put food on the table, Your Grace."

"I understand, but artistic tastes change. That is why His Holiness has granted you a lifetime income, in recognition of your contributions to our culture. He has also provided you and your staff with exceptional accommodations within the Vatican."

"But—"

"And now I must attend another meeting."

Walking down a vast marble concourse, Leonardo looked like a lonely, humbled, white-bearded old man. A pair of young artists approached, chatting with a cardinal.

"We shall make it a grand mural, Your Grace, illustrating the Passion of Our Savior!" one of the artists exclaimed.

The other noticed Leonardo, then murmured, "Who's that?"

The first softly replied, "Too old to be Michelangelo. Could it be Leonardo?"

"Isn't he dead?"

The cardinal spoke. "No, he's not dead. They pensioned off the old codger to the Belvedere."

Leonardo heard every word, and each one stung. He was only sixty-two. When the artists and the cardinal passed, he looked after them as they strolled down the concourse.

"So I pass, almost forgotten, into history," he said to himself. With a bitter smile, he continued on his way.

Back at the Belvedere, Leonardo immediately noted Francesco's sad face.

"What is it?" he asked anxiously, though he already knew.

"Donato is gone," Francesco said, his eyes filling with tears.

"Why didn't they warn me?" Leonardo cried. "I would have come instantly!"

"Maestro, Donato asked yesterday that a message be sent to you. But we never received it."

"He was *waiting* for me?" This was too much for Leonardo to bear, and he collapsed to the floor. "I'll never talk to him again! I'll never laugh with him, or break bread with him! I have nothing left! Anything I love, I lose!"

Leonardo remained inconsolable. Francesco could do nothing for him the rest of the day and through the long night.

Chapter Twenty-Three

A MEETING WITH THE POPE

It was a windy, chilly night in Rome. In the Ospedale San Spirito, a morgue attendant stood nervously before the hospital director. Ugo, the attendant, was used to dead bodies, not live ones. "When I came upon him in the morgue," he was saying, "he had half of the skull cut away and was probing deep inside the brain." He paused and shifted his feet.

"Go on," the director said.

"I asked him what he was looking for. He answered that if he knew, he wouldn't be looking. I don't understand him. He has been here almost every night for the past two weeks, and he makes a mess. Organs, and drawings of organs, everywhere. At first, his assistant did his best to clean up. But he became ill from the work and now stays behind at the Vatican."

The director waited for Ugo to continue.

"I come to you out of confusion," the attendant said. "Leonardo is a painter. He is not a doctor or a professor. His dissections serve no purpose, unless he is doing the Devil's work. It is some kind of black magic or witchcraft? I'm a religious man, Direttore. I go to mass. I make confession. I want nothing to do with any of that."

After a long silence, the director cleared his throat. "I appreciate your coming to me, Ugo. The reputation of this hospital, and even our own salvation, are at stake. I order you not to speak with anyone else about this."

"*Certo*, Direttore!" Ugo vowed. He hoped he had seen the last of the painter and his scalpels.

Days later, on a bright morning, Leonardo and Francesco were assembling a scale model of a dam when Salai entered and handed Leonardo a note.

"A message from the Vatican Palace," he announced. "The pope requires your presence."

Leonardo's eyes widened. "Finally! A commission!"

An hour later, in the Papal apartments, a robed functionary escorted Leonardo through several doorways and pairs of Swiss guards to a private audience room. Leonardo sat in a chair while the functionary knocked on another door. In a few moments, it opened, revealing a cardinal. The two of them spoke in low tones. The cardinal looked darkly at Leonardo, said a few words to the functionary, and closed the door.

That look sent Leonardo's mind spinning. What had he done? Had he committed a transgression against the Holy See?

A few moments later, the door opened again, and this time Pope Leo X strode into the room, followed by the cardinal. Leo would be the last pope to come from the secular world and not from a religious order. To finance his basilica for St. Peter, he had granted indulgences to shady merchants and bankers. He considered himself a benefactor of the arts.

Leonardo knelt on one knee and kissed his ring.

"I am honored to meet you and grateful for your generosity, Your Holiness. How may I serve you?"

The pontiff sat in a chair and leveled a steely gaze at Leonardo. "Please, sit," he said. The cardinal took a seat in a corner of the room.

"Thank you, Your Holiness." Leonardo sat across from him.

"We will get right to the point," the pope said.

Leonardo felt a bead of sweat form on his forehead. With one word, the man across from him could sweep away his livelihood and the roof over his head.

"We are greatly concerned about you, Leonardo. You have been in Rome only a short time, but already the director of the Ospedale San Spirito has complained to the Holy See about your late-night dissections of human bodies. He has inferred that you are practicing witchcraft."

Leonardo was speechless.

The pope went on. "Two people have accused you of black magic, one at the Ospedale's morgue, and one other."

"Who makes these false accusations?" Leonardo wanted to know.

"The mirror-maker Giovanni has said that you practice sorcery during your dissections at the hospital."

"Giovanni tried to steal my designs for the mirror I wish to build. It can be used to view the stars with great detail, or even to harness the power of the sun. I swear to Your Holiness that I have never practiced sorcery or even contemplated it."

"Then why do you do your dissections?"

"I study anatomy to better understand the human body as a painter, sculptor, and scientist," Leonardo explained. "Some of my research could aid the efforts of doctors to extend the human lifespan."

The pope raised an eyebrow. "Please explain."

"In the corpses of older men who died after experiencing severe pain in the chest, I found that the insides of the arteries leading from their hearts contained a gritty substance."

"That is all very interesting, but the fact remains that you are dissecting human bodies."

"Yes, Your Holiness. For science and art."

"We will tell the mirror-maker to stop making false accusations," the pope said. "But you must also stop dissecting bodies. It's unnatural, unclean, and ungodly." The pope leaned forward in his chair for emphasis. "It would be wise of you to confine your research to activities that cannot, under any circumstance, be construed as witchcraft."

It was then that Leo noticed how closely the cardinal was listening.

"It is only a matter of time before the inquisitors become active in Rome," Leo said. "We have fought them because we do not believe that torture leads to credible confessions. It is ungodly, and to torture in the name of the church is a very great sin. And to burn the sinners afterward means certain damnation. The inquisitors accuse others of consorting with demons, yet their own witch burnings are pagan rites."

Leo sighed. He was tired of fighting a very long battle. "Our predecessors in the Holy City long since granted the inquisitors power and influence in France, Spain, Portugal, and even in the New World. Earnest prayer, confession, and good works are all one needs to enter heaven, but even our Roman faithful seem to favor the excesses of these butchers."

The pope looked sternly at Leonardo. "If word of your dissections reaches the inquisitors' ears ahead of their arrival in Rome, your name will be added to their list, and you will certainly be interrogated. And you will not survive. We have spoken to you today in great confidence, and you must tell no one of our discussion. Do you agree?"

"Yes, Your Holiness."

"We say these things because we care for you. God has given you and your works to us as treasures to hold dear for all the ages to come. The Father, the Son, and the Holy Spirit work through you, my son, in ways that you cannot even imagine. We order you to stop the dissections immediately. We will issue an edict with which you must comply or face the consequences."

For a long moment, the room was completely silent. Leonardo knew that he was dangerously close to excommunication. Suddenly, a robin chirped outside the open window. Leonardo spoke, gently and quietly.

"Your Holiness, I will hold in strict confidence what you have told me. But I beg your indulgence, for this reason: I think it is right to study the works of God, who created so many marvelous things. For man to acquire such knowledge reveals God's greatness. Everything we see has been created by the Lord. Studying such things is surely a way to become closer to God—"

Leo interrupted, "Enough! You have ventured too near heresy. Man becoming closer to God? There is only one way to do that, the way prescribed by the canons and dogma of the church and the edicts of the Holy See!"

"Holy Father, if I have offended you—"

"You offend God, Signore! Speak no more of this, to me or to anyone, or you will bring damnation on your soul!"

The cardinal in the corner looked concerned. He had never seen the pontiff so upset. Leo managed to calm himself, then continued.

"You are a brave man, Leonardo, to stand up to our scrutiny and censure. But you are also stubborn. You have done your research, as you call it, and now you must cease. Word about Giovanni's accusation has spread within the Vatican and will surely spread beyond our walls unless you comply. We cannot and must not look foolish to the other cardinals. There are very unpleasant ways of replacing a pope. We forbid you to continue!"

Leonardo noticed that the pope's face was very red. He had said what he needed to say. He had been true to himself and spoken his heart and mind. That was all he could do.

The pope wasn't quite finished with him. "You are officially banned from human dissections. Should you violate our edict, we will be forced to excommunicate you from the church." With that, Pope Leo rose and left the room, with the cardinal close behind. The door closed with finality.

Chapter Twenty-Four

THE NIGHTMARE

Leonardo worked in his Belvedere studio on a painting of *St. John the Baptist*. Meanwhile, Francesco drew Leonardo's face in profile.

"You're not drawing me again, are you?" Leonardo wanted to know.

"I'm almost finished."

"You should get a younger model."

"Then it wouldn't be you, Maestro."

Leonardo was silent.

"No one has commissioned you to paint Saint John," Francesco continued. "Why are you drawn to him? Was it his prophecy of the coming of Christ?"

"Indeed. It leads me to wonder what I should predict before I leave this earth."

"Please, Maestro! You have many years—"

"Why should I have many years? There's nothing in Rome for me now, except to follow Giuliano de' Medici, digging trenches and building mounds. This was not the life I had in mind."

Leonardo put down his brush, stepped back from the painting, and studied it. "Why does man finish one war, then immediately start planning another?"

"I don't know, Maestro. But I'm confused by your Saint John. Is he prophesying Christ's coming? Is that why he points to the sky?"

"I don't know. Don't think about it. What does your heart tell you?"

Francesco didn't answer.

"I'll tell you what I do know," Leonardo said. "I know there is something more to life than the getting and spending of money. Something more than houses, lands, and other possessions. Man is meant for finer, higher things than the gold chains and ruby pendants to be found on the Ponte Vecchio."

"Of course. Man is meant for heaven. That is the higher, finer thing."

"Possibly, yes."

"Maestro! You must not say such things in public, or write them in your notebooks. They would be seen as heresy."

"That is one reason I write my notes backwards, and in reverse," Leonardo said. "Have you ever known me to speak thus in public?"

Francesco shook his head.

"And you never will, now that I have been scolded by the pope."

"That's not fair, Maestro. He seems like a fair man."

"But the church is not fair. It grinds men in its gears."

Both men returned to work, and for a time, the studio was silent except for the sounds of Leonardo's brush and Paolo's charcoal. Then Francesco impulsively asked, "Maestro, why do you paint?"

Leonardo thought for a moment.

"Because beauty awakens the soul. And neither popes nor kings, princes nor condottieri can quell my desire to know its true nature."

"But why bother, when others are content to pray for salvation of their souls?"

"I'm not like others, Francesco. Sometimes I wish I were."

Suddenly, his brush felt too heavy to hold. Leonardo put it down again and lay on a couch. "My apologies, Francesco," he said. "The model must withdraw temporarily."

Francesco watched him in silence. He felt guilty for Leonardo's dark mood.

Leonardo stared idly at the ceiling. It started to rain, and the light faded from the studio. He remembered the solar eclipse in Milan long ago, during the Black Death. He felt he was entering a night of the soul that was darker still.

The next morning, Leonardo awoke from a terrifying and familiar nightmare. He called for Francesco. In a few moments, Francesco opened the door to his room and rushed in.

"Maestro, are you all right?"

"The dream came again. I thought the world was ending! Do you think the end is coming? Or is it simply my end?"

Francesco didn't know what to say.

"I can't get the images out of my mind," Leonardo said.

"Then paint them. Share them to rid yourself of these demons."

"I will tell them to you. Write them down for me."

Francesco went in search of pen and paper. Returning, he sat in a chair.

Leonardo began.

"I see tremendous waves from a powerful storm in the Alps. They flood farms and cities alike. They swallow whole ships and their crews. The air swirls violently and mixes with rain, hail, and broken trees. Mountains collapse into valleys strewn with trees uprooted by the wind."

Francesco wrote at a furious pace.

"The surge of water covers whole valleys, including all the life within: men, women, children, and terrified animals, both wild and domesticated. Tables, beds, boats, even houses race by in the wild currents. Families huddle on top of anything that still floats. They stare in terror at the corpses swirling past them."

Leonardo wiped his eyes.

"They pray. They scream. They cry to God for mercy. But there is no quarter given, nor any mercy shown."

Leonardo looked at Francesco, whose face was wet with tears.

"Wailing wolves, foxes, snakes, horses, sheep, and cows, forgetting their natural enmity, crowd together on whatever remains above the water, however small. They stare with wide, terrified eyes at the drowned."

He shuddered. "This is my dream, night after night! The destruction of all living things."

"You must paint it, Maestro," Francesco said.

Leonardo wasn't through yet.

"Men fire or thrust what weapons they have salvaged, defending their pitiful refuges from the lions, wolves, and other savage beasts seeking shelter. Others cover their ears against the violent winds that fill the air with wet clouds and debris. They shield their children from the thunderbolts that flash eerie light on the death throes of innocent creatures."

Leonardo sat up in bed and rested his head in his hands. "Some strangle themselves with their own hands. They seize their own children and kill them. Mothers howl curses at the heavens as they weep for the drowned sons they hold in their laps, like the Pieta!"

Leonardo stood and put on a coat. "Before I start painting, I will draw studies in black lead, befitting the subject matter. The final deluge. The end of all life on earth. There will be no Ark of Noah to save any living thing."

Francesco made a sigh like a death rattle. He put down his pen and flexed his sore fingers, then looked at Leonardo with red-rimmed eyes.

"I'm sorry, Francesco," Leonardo said. "I seem to want to bring everyone and everything down to the level of my useless life."

"It's only a dream, Maestro."

"Then why does it return again and again, like a prophecy?"

"I don't know. What I do know is this: You are my ark. If not for you, I would have had a boring career in the military that would have amounted to nothing. Like my father, I would have been a frustrated painter."

"At least I have done one good thing," Leonardo said.

Weeks later, Leonardo surveyed a long table covered with drawings of his nightmare. Violent destruction was a common theme. Terrified faces and children struggling to keep their heads above water. Animals bloated and flailing. Houses, trees, and mountains collapsing.

Francesco approached Leonardo, holding a drawing.

"You have finally finished my profile?" Leonardo asked.

Francesco nervously nodded.

"Then let me see it."

"You won't like it."

"For God's sake, Francesco! No one cares whether I like it or not!"

"But I do!" Francesco protested. Reluctantly, he placed his drawing face up on the table.

Leonardo looked at it for a long time. Finally, he gave a small sigh of satisfaction.

"This drawing, and the paintings you have done in my studio, are masterful works," he said. "You have learned much and will have a career of your own when I am gone."

"Please, Maestro, don't!"

"I can't possibly be that noble," Leonardo said, indicating the drawing. "It's not really me, is it?"

"It is only you."

Later that week, Leonardo was finishing his *St. John the Baptist* painting while Francesco touched up another one. Leonardo became thoughtful as he studied his work.

"I believe that Saint John succeeded in reaching the limits of human knowledge," he said. "Not faith. Knowledge. That's what enabled him to foretell the coming of the Christ. It is why I painted that look in his eyes. But the more I study his eyes, the more jealous I become. And why does he smile? Be honest, Francesco. Wouldn't you like to know?"

Chapter Twenty-Five

SEEKING PEACE

Perched on top of one of Rome's seven hills, Giuliano de' Medici's palazzo was grand, with large grounds. On a day in 1515, Leonardo arrived by coach and paid the driver. He wasn't easily impressed by the garish palazzos of the wealthy and powerful, but he was impressed by this one, a testament to the fine taste of its owner.

Leonardo had come to congratulate his friend on his upcoming marriage. But as soon as he stepped inside the foyer, Medici's personal secretary tried to get rid of him. "My master is getting married in France," the secretary insisted. "His departure is imminent. He has no time for visitors."

Medici heard their voices and called to Leonardo from the second-floor landing. "Come up!" he called. "Quickly! I need your opinion."

Leonardo climbed the stairs to Medici's apartments and found him standing before a full-length mirror, evaluating his outfit. The secretary slipped in behind him and stood to one side.

"What do you think, Maestro?" Medici asked. "Will this help me recapture Filiberta's heart after an absence of several months?"

"Love, Your Excellency?" Leonardo asked. "I thought this was an arranged marriage."

"It is, but…well…we have fallen in love! Is that so surprising?"

"I cannot speak of affairs of the heart with any authority, but I can give you an artist's evaluation of your attire."

"Then go on, and hurry!"

Leonardo looked him up and down before saying, "Everything is fine—"

"Wonderful! Then—"

"—except the shoes."

Medici looked confused. "But my tailor said—"

"I know. The shoes are brown, like your pants. But they are a different shade of brown. In relation to the pants, they are the wrong brown."

"Nicolo!" The secretary jumped. "Bring me all of my brown shoes! We should have been on the road two hours ago. And, in my absence, find me a new tailor!"

A half-hour later, Leonardo bid farewell to Medici at the door.

"I wish you a wonderful trip, Your Excellency, and an even more wonderful wedding."

"Thank you, my friend," Medici said. "When I return, you will design my new armor. There is no telling what the French will do next. While I marry the daughter of one of their dukes, they could be planning their next invasion across the Alps!"

Medici's joke turned out to be prophetic. Weeks later, Leonardo learned that Louis XII had died and King Francis I had begun reassembling his armies. Once more, Leonardo was summoned to the Vatican.

Leonardo crossed St. Peter's square, wondering what the Vatican could possibly want with him. He hadn't touched a scalpel since meeting with the pope. As he entered the Vatican Palace, Swiss guards brought him swiftly to the office of Sebastiano Fratinelli, the Apostolic nuncio to France.

Fratinelli was an archbishop, and his office was large, luxurious, and well-appointed. Leonardo could almost see his own reflection in the polished wood-paneled walls, and shelves held many rare and expensive books.

A man in his early sixties, tall and thin, entered through another door. Fratinelli greeted Leonardo and gestured toward a pair of chairs. When the two men sat, an attendant poured wine, then stood in a corner, ready for requests.

Fratinelli wasted no time. "The French have invaded Lombardy under the command of their new king. As the pope's representative to France, I feel the weight of history on my shoulders. But it rests even more heavily on the shoulders of His Holiness. He and I wish to share some of that weight with you."

Leonardo was puzzled. "Your Excellency, the affairs of state are beyond me. I have never involved myself—"

"Nevertheless," Fratinelli interrupted, "I'll tell you what we need from you, and you'll tell me if you can do it."

"Yes, Your Excellency."

Fratinelli stood up and paced as he spoke. "We have received new information from our network of messengers. From this, we can surmise the intentions of the French king."

He paused. Leonardo waited patiently.

"Once he crossed the Alps and entered Lombardy," Fratinelli said, "our armies met his at Marignano, where most of our men died under his artillery fire and at the ends of his lances. In a few days, he had captured Milan."

"My God!" Leonardo said, shaking his head. "I have seen Milan fall before, Your Excellency."

"We know you have, and we know your experience on the battlefield with Borgia."

"When will all this empire-building and needless bloodshed end?" Leonardo cried.

"Only when the Day of Judgment comes, my son. Until then, the lands we love will be subject to the aggressive caprices of kings and princes. After Marignano, many more Italian troops, including our Papal armies, were sent against the French. They, too, were soundly defeated."

Fratinelli's face reddened. "Full of Gallic pride and bloodlust, the French have been unstoppable. Our staff talks of nothing but the danger King Francis poses to our Mother Church."

Leonardo didn't understand what any of this had to do with him. "What do you need from me, Your Excellency?"

"The Holy Father respects you and believes that your art can be a force for peace. He is well acquainted with your skills as a painter. Through the Holy Father's brother, Giuliano de' Medici, we are also aware of your advanced engineering and mechanical accomplishments."

Leonardo was puzzled. Did the pope want him to paint something or build something?

"His Holiness has invited me to join him for peace negotiations in Bologna with King Francis, so that no more blood is spilled on either side," Fratinelli said.

"Finally! Positive news!" Leonardo responded. "I am acquainted with the horrors of war, and I stand ready to be of whatever service I can render to you and His Holiness, so that peace can be achieved as soon as possible. I live for nothing more than to see man in harmony with himself, with others, and with nature. Please, tell me what I can do for you."

Fratinelli stopped pacing and returned to his chair. "His Holiness desires you to complete a particular commission. Through our agents in the French court, we know that Francis's sister, Marguerite de Navarre, has influenced her brother to be tolerant of this new, heretical, and dangerous Protestant movement. We also know that Francis is merely using the Protestants for his own ends. By tolerating these heretics, he has successfully wooed many German princes away from allegiance to his sworn enemy, the Holy Roman Emperor."

Leonardo listened closely. He was learning more about European politics in this one interview than he had in a long time—information that could serve him well in planning his own future.

"Given the military and political situation in Europe," Fratinelli went on, "if we do not deal effectively with Francis at the diplomatic level, this could spell an end to the safety of our Mother Church." Francis suddenly seemed distracted. "Forgive me. I get hungry when I worry. May I offer you a refreshment?"

"That's kind of you to ask," Leonardo said. "Yes, please."

Fratinelli beckoned to the attendant waiting patiently in the corner.

"Domenico, have some roast pheasant sent up. Also some cheeses and fruits."

"Yes, Your Excellency."

Returning to Leonardo, Fratinelli said, "King Francis has a love for the arts and a great respect for Florentine painting and sculpture. We are allied with Florence in an effort to contain this fearless French lion." He leaned forward for emphasis. "His Holiness would like you to create a playful mechanical device that draws its inspiration from the historic friendship between Florence and France. Something using the lion, symbol of Florence, and the fleur-de-lis, representing France."

"Brilliant!" Leonardo responded. His mind raced ahead on creative and mechanical levels, already calculating materials and labor costs.

Fratinelli smiled. "Then you are willing?"

"I would love to do this for you, for the Holy Father and for Rome!" Leonardo exclaimed. "I wish I had thought of it myself."

"Knowing your reputation, you probably would have, in time. But time is a luxury we do not have."

"Then I shall begin immediately."

Fratinelli stood, as did Leonardo. "We want your full-time, wholehearted best efforts on this device, for which you will be well paid," Fratinelli said. "You must design and fabricate it with great haste. We leave soon for the conference in Bologna."

"We?"

"You will personally present this gift to King Francis, on behalf of His Holiness and the Florentine and Roman states."

Leonardo was speechless. Never had he been offered such an honor and given such responsibility. He felt the weight of history on his own shoulders. When the food arrived, Leonardo had already gone.

Leonardo hurried back to the Belvedere and entered his apartments in a blind rush, calling Francesco's name. Francesco soon appeared, and Leonardo commanded, "Come with me!" They went through the library and study into the studio, which was filled with paintings in progress, mechanical inventions, and drawings hanging on walls and unrolled on large tables.

"Clear the studio!" Leonardo ordered.

"What's happening?" Francesco wanted to know.

"Just do it!" He looked around, then shouted for Salai, who had been sleeping out of sight in a corner. Salai stood up, rubbing his eyes. "Why so much noise?"

"Help Francesco clear the studio!" Leonardo said. "You can begin by rolling the drawings on the table."

He whirled to face Francesco. "Send messengers immediately. Have them hire two metal fabricators and one assembler of machine parts, since my left arm pains me."

Within days, Leonardo had designed a large mechanical device and hung a large drawing on a wall. Pointing to the drawing with his left arm, then wincing and switching to his right, Leonardo led his new team in a cheer for victory over the French king's onslaught on the peninsula.

They all worked together at a high rate of speed to build it. Fueled by a sense of urgency—and the bonuses Leonardo had promised—they skipped celebrating the Feast of St. Michael in late September. Everyone was on board for the future of their independent Rome, and they loved working for Leonardo on such a cause. Even Salai had warmed to his tasks.

Day after day and into the night, the studio was charged with energy. Leonardo had food brought in. There was always a table in his study laden with whatever his staff desired. At meals, they laughed and joked, and Leonardo serenaded them on his lute. When he called an end to the meal break, they scrambled back to work.

One day, Leonardo walked around the studio, watching as two assistants cut large pieces of metal and a third assembled gears for the inner workings of the device. He kicked a metal scrap under a table and observed the progress in the room. He smiled at Francesco, who was amazed by the activity.

On the sixth day, everyone gathered in the center of the studio. An assistant pulled the draping cloth off a large shape underneath. There stood a metal lion, ferocious-looking and seemingly poised to lunge. It was a daunting creation, and it was theirs. They cheered in one voice, as men who knew they had accomplished something important, something big, in a small amount of time.

"To peace!" Leonardo yelled.

"To peace!" they shouted as one.

"Congratulations, gentlemen!" Leonard said, overflowing with love and gratitude. "We've done it! Tomorrow morning, Leonardo of Vinci and the Nuncio for France will follow the pope to Bologna." He put his hand on the lion's side. "I pray that this machine will help us to bring peace with France. I could never have done this without your help. And we will all be well paid by the Vatican! Even you, Salai."

Everyone laughed. Salai, for the first time in his life, looked both embarrassed and pleased.

Chapter Twenty-Six

THE FRENCH KING

The Bologna peace conference was held in September 1516 in the Palazzo d'Accursio in the center of the city. Soldiers of both sides were bivouacked on the expansive Piazza Maggiore that faced the palazzo. French and Italian tents had been raised on the paving stones, with their respective colors flying in the breeze.

The conference took place in a spacious inner courtyard. Diplomats, dignitaries, Pope Leo, several cardinals, and military officers of both armies sat around a long, rectangular conference table. Papers were continually passed among them. Behind the pope stood a half-dozen Swiss guards.

On the other side of the table, facing the pope, sat King Francis I of France. Behind him stood several armed soldiers. Francis wore a highly decorated uniform with a royal ribbon-and-medal across his chest.

On opposite edges of the courtyard were two unoccupied thrones. Not far from one of the thrones, two soldiers—one French, one Italian—helped Leonardo position a large object covered with a cloth. Completing the task, they stood guard on either side.

Absentmindedly rubbing his left arm, Leonardo turned to look at the conference table. Fratinelli approached. "Leonardo, we'll be ready for the unveiling as soon as Francis leaves the table," he said.

Leonardo nodded. He was ready.

Moments later, the conference attendees took a break. Most of them stood and dispersed. Others gathered in small groups for conversations in the courtyard or out on the piazza. Francis remained seated to discuss something with one of his generals.

Fratinelli had a few words with Francis, who got up from the table and crossed the courtyard to sit on his throne. French noblemen and officers followed and gathered around him. This was the signal for the pope to move to his throne. Between the two stood Leonardo and his creation, still covered, accompanied by soldiers.

Fratinelli spoke to Francis in a voice loud enough to be heard by all. "Your Highness, we have brought a gift for you that demonstrates the bond between Florence and France."

"Then undrape the thing," Francis said. "I've been trying all day to guess what it is."

Fratinelli beckoned Leonardo to come closer.

"Your Highness, may I present to you the renowned painter, inventor, and military engineer, Ser Leonardo da Vinci."

Leonardo bowed slightly and looked into Francis's intelligent eyes. The man was all neck, with slightly puffy cheeks and a well-trimmed but unattractive beard. "Your Highness, it's a very great honor to meet you," he said. "I hope you will enjoy our gift to you."

"I hope so too," Francis said, smiling. It seemed that he and Leonardo were off to a good start.

With a flourish, Leonardo unveiled his lion.

Francis was delighted.

"How intriguing! The lion is Florence?"

"Yes, Your Highness."

The king's guards eyed it warily.

Leonardo touched something on the lion and stepped back. Suddenly, to the astonishment of everyone present, the lion moved. Gasps were heard as it began walking toward the king. Francis was fascinated. His guards held their lances at the ready.

But the wonders were only beginning. After walking six feet on its own, the lion sat back on its hind legs. Its chest opened. From inside the chest, a fleur-de-lis emerged—the symbol of France.

King Francis laughed and clapped. Others followed his lead. "*Fantastique!*" he exclaimed. "It is out of a dream! You have made this for me?"

"Yes, Your Highness," Leonardo responded. "On behalf of His Holiness the Pope and the people of Florence and Rome."

"*C'est parfait!*" the king exclaimed. He nodded in acknowledgment to the pope, who nodded back.

Francis addressed his entourage. "With such great spirit and graciousness as our Italian friends have shown us today, we certainly hope, and put our faith in God, that in these meetings we will establish an equitable and lasting peace that will put an end to the current hostilities."

There were murmurs of approval from both the French and Italians.

Francis continued. "Leonardo, I have heard a great deal about your accomplishments from my late uncle, King Louis, may God rest his soul. That you are a genius in more than one field is plain to see."

"Thank you, Your Highness. I'm gratified that you like my work."

"Then do me the honor of attending me in my tent." Francis rose from his throne. Accompanied by his guards, he left the courtyard.

Fratinelli appeared at Leonardo's side. "Congratulations!" he beamed. "What a success! You have marvelously had the desired effect on King Francis. His Holiness is very pleased."

King Francis I and Pope Leo X had the only two tents in the courtyard. Everyone else had to sleep outside in the piazza or upstairs in makeshift apartments in spare offices.

The interior of King Francis's tent was opulently decorated and furnished. Tapestries hung between the tent poles. Bear rugs and cushions covered the courtyard's paving stones. The odors of the city of Bologna were masked by bowls and bouquets of lilies, violets, and jasmine.

Francis and Leonardo sat on couches while servants brought roast duckling, wines, cheeses, fruits, breads, and biscotti.

Francis spoke first. "The lion is most impressive."

"Thank you, Your Highness. I have had many significant commissions in Florence, Milan, and Rome, but my focus in recent years has been more on inner adventures than outer ones."

"I have been told that you pay scant attention to what your patrons desire. Instead, you concentrate your efforts on discovering what you call ultimate truth. Is that correct?"

Leonardo smiled. "Yes, Your Highness. I am guilty of the sin of leaving many projects unfinished. Once I have fully envisioned them in my mind, I sometimes lose interest in completing them."

"That's of no concern to me. Your focus is precisely why I want to bring you to France." Francis could see that Leonardo was astonished. "I, too, am interested in the inner adventures," he continued. "I have already fully experienced the outer ones, from the softness of a woman's thigh to the hard steel of a sword blade."

The artist and the king had a good, long talk. Later, Francis and one of his advisors, Henri de Mesnières, watched Leonardo walk away from the tent.

"My contacts at the Vatican tell me that Monsieur Léonard, while his genius in the arts and sciences is immensely respected across the entire region, is underutilized in Rome," Francis said. "Instead of being richly rewarded with commissions, he has been shunted aside for younger artists."

"That is correct, Your Highness."

"For a man of his accomplishments, it's not only inappropriate, it's ridiculous. We shall have him at our court!"

The two men walked back inside the tent, where Francis grabbed a leg of duck and bit into it with relish.

"As Our Lord Jesus Christ said, a prophet is not honored in his own hometown," Mesnières commented.

"The time is right to bring the spirit of the Renaissance to our homeland," Francis said. "Make Monsieur Léonard an appropriately generous offer. But not too soon. We don't want to seem desperate to have him at Amboise."

Several weeks later, Leonardo lay on his side in his bedroom at the Belvedere, staring with a mixture of sadness and fascination at his *Mona Lisa*, when he heard Francesco shout his name from the foyer. With the sound of running footsteps, Francesco burst into the room. He handed a sealed envelope to Leonardo and said with excitement, "A messenger from King Francis awaits your reply!"

Leonardo broke the seal. He pulled out the letter and said, "It's from the king's advisor, Mesnières." He read aloud.

Monsieur Léonard, it is my great pleasure to inform you that, for the purposes of advancing the arts and sciences in the Kingdom of France, His Highness François Premier invites you and your closest staff to permanently relocate, as his guests, to the Royal Court in Amboise.

For this honor you would bestow on him, you will be paid a large salary, and your staff will also be compensated. You will have the free use of the entire estate of the Château de Cloux, which is very near the royal palace.

Leonardo looked up at Francesco in amazement. Meanwhile, Salai had walked into the room and was listening intently. Leonardo spoke. "My God, Francesco. We are saved!"

Suddenly, Leonardo was overcome by ambivalence. On the one hand, this was a tremendous offer from the reigning King of France. On the other, he was being asked to leave the homeland he loved. But was there anything here for him, in Rome or elsewhere in Italy? Clearly, he would need time to think.

Weeks passed before Henri de Mesnières sat at his desk in the French court of Amboise, reading a letter from Rome.

Cher Monsieur de Mesnières,

Please convey to His Highness my most sincere gratitude for his very generous and attractive offer. Out of loyalty to my current patron, Giuliano de' Medici, I have decided to stay at the Vatican for the time being.

Henri put Leonardo's letter down on his desk and spoke out loud to himself. "Hmmm. 'For the time being.' I wonder what that means?" He smiled.

Months went by at the Belvedere as Leonardo worked on a new design for a large building. One day, Francesco entered, looking downcast.

"I've been to the pope's retainer for news of Giuliano," he said. "A messenger arrived from Florence today. Giuliano has only a few days to live."

Leonardo put down his pen and protested. "He's only thirty-seven years old!"

"The fever came on suddenly, without warning."

Leonardo rested his head in his hands. For several minutes, he said nothing. Then he raised his head and spoke.

"I have long been weary of Milan's political instability, and the Signoria of Florence would not welcome us. So, my friend, for the next few months, why don't we, in our graciousness and generosity, give Rome the opportunity to bestow another patron on us? Despite the fact that Michelangelo, Raphael, and Titian are winning all the significant commissions?"

"And if no patron comes forward?" Francesco asked.

"*Parlez-vous Français, Monsieur?*"

Some months later, on an afternoon in early September 1516, nobles came and went, conversing with one another, in the gardens of the French royal palace at Amboise. Inside the palace, Francis sat in deep concentration in his office, writing a poem. Two greyhounds sat at his feet, looking up at him expectantly.

He casually tossed them bits of beef from a bowl. They caught them in mid-air and waited for more.

Henri de Mesnières entered and cleared his throat.

"Henri!" Francis exclaimed. "I have written another poem. Would you like to hear it?"

"Of course, Your Highness. Would you like to hear some news from Italy?"

Francis raised an eyebrow.

"We today received a note from Leonardo of Vinci. He has accepted your offer."

"We'll dispense with my poetry for the moment," Francis said, smiling. "He is a much greater gift to France. What else did he say?"

"That he has decided never to return to Italy."

"I don't blame him. Anything else?"

Henri looked down at the letter. "He will bring all his paintings, drawings, inventions, and other objects, and many thousands of pages of notes on all manner of aesthetic, scientific, and philosophic subjects."

"Wonderful news, Henri! This is a coup for French culture. Leonardo will augment our own Renaissance!"

"And bring an end forever to the dark days of ignorance!"

"Speak to my Chief of Estates," Francis commanded. "Have the designers and workmen go through the Château de Cloux thoroughly, to ensure the Maestro finds everything to his liking. The Master of the Household must find other accommodations in the palace for my dear sister."

"Yes, Your Highness."

"A journey across the Alps, with several wagonloads of property? That's a dangerous, difficult trip for a young man, let alone an older one. Write to him that we will send a small troop contingent and several strong, covered conveyances to safely escort him, his staff, and all of their possessions across the mountains."

"I will see to all of this immediately, Your Highness."

Francis added, "They must cross the Alps before the first snows of November. We can't have the greatest thinker in Europe lying frozen in a snowdrift, to be discovered in the spring with his arms wrapped around his paintings!"

Many weeks later, just below a ridge on an Alpine road, a French troop contingent rested, along with Leonardo, Francesco, Salai, and a new servant, Luca Battista, who was in his twenties and strong. Several wagons nearby were stuffed with Leonardo's worldly goods. The snows had not yet come, but everyone was bundled against the autumn cold at that altitude.

From the top of the ridge, an excited officer called to Leonardo. "Monsieur Léonard, if you please, come and see this!" With beautiful vistas all around him, Leonardo felt no need of more. Still, huffing and puffing, he climbed the short distance to where the officer stood. On the way, he joked with himself. "Maybe this soldier has found the ultimate truth!"

The officer pointed to a high mountain in the distance. "There is Mont Blanc, Monsieur. It is the highest peak in the Alps." He noticed how weary Leonardo looked. "Take heart! We are almost in France. Another week and a half and we'll be in the Valley of the Loire and Amboise, at last."

Chapter Twenty-Seven

FROM ITALY TO FRANCE

The days went by, and Leonardo and the others entered a deep forest in the Loire Valley of central France. The caravan passed dense stands of pines that lined the road. Turning onto a long, private drive, they followed it toward a large manor house in the distance. When they reached a courtyard, the troops dismounted to stretch their legs.

Leonardo and his staff looked admiringly at the lovely three-story home. Francesco helped Leonardo down from their wagon. Henri de Mesnières emerged from the front entrance, followed by a smiling man and woman.

"Monsieur Léonard! Welcome to Château de Cloux! I am Henri de Mesnières, the King's advisor for international cultural affairs. I was at the Bologna conference but missed you. It's wonderful to finally meet you! Allow us to help with the unloading." He turned to the man and woman and spoke in French. They headed toward the wagons.

"Those are your cook and your groundskeeper, Monsieur," Mesnières said. "I am sure you will find that both are excellent. They are paid by the French crown. King Francis is very excited to have you here and will visit later. The palace is near the château. I am here to see that everything meets with your satisfaction."

Mesnières finally took a breath, and Leonardo said, "*Merci beaucoup, Monsieur Mesnières. C'est ma plaisir faire votre connaissance et aussi d'etre en Amboise.*"

"Ahhh! *Votre Français est tres bien!*"

Leonardo laughed. "I became somewhat familiar with your language while working for Charles d'Amboise and his staff in Milan. And I've been practicing lately, although I don't expect to achieve much fluency this late in life."

"But, Monsieur, you are certainly off to a good start. It's not mandatory, of course. I speak Italian, German, English, and Spanish, as well as French. We are overjoyed to have you here, and many of our staff speak Italian, of course, as does His Highness, as you know from the Bologna conference."

Leonardo suddenly noticed that two soldiers had propped the *Mona Lisa* against a wall of the château. "Please excuse me, Henri. I must ensure the safety and placement of my three favorite paintings."

"But of course!"

Before long, Leonardo was sitting at a handsome desk in his well-appointed bedroom. He and Henri watched as Francesco set the *Mona Lisa* on an easel. Beside her, on their own easels, rested the *Virgin and Child with St. Anne* and *St. John the Baptist*. Mesnières looked from one to the other in awe.

"I am speechless, Monsieur Leonardo. All are great masterpieces. Their arrival here is a historic moment for France."

"*Merci bien*, Henri," Leonardo said. "It is even more historic for me."

"Now that they are situated, permit me to show you your new home. With your staff, so all will know their way around."

Leonardo, Francesco, Salai, and Battista followed Mesnières through the many rooms of the manor. Leonardo noticed a closed door at the end of one hallway.

"What is this room?" he wanted to know.

"Be careful," Mesnières warned. "It is the door to a stairway that leads to a tunnel, and it requires a lantern to negotiate. The tunnel connects the château to the palace. It is very likely the route the King will use to visit you."

Promising a later tour of the grounds, Mesnières led Leonardo and his staff back to their rooms. "I would speak to you in private, Maestro," Mesnières said. Leonardo dismissed his staff, then turned expectantly to the King's advisor.

"Along with the use of this estate," Mesnières began, "His Highness has granted you a large annual fee, with no obligation on your part to execute any commissions. You have spent your lifetime working on paintings and other projects chosen for you. The King wishes to grant you the freedom to choose for yourself. You may create what you like, or nothing at all."

Leonardo was overcome with gratitude. "Please express my great appreciation to His Majesty," he said.

Mesnières continued. "Francesco, your chief assistant, will also be given a salary. Salai and Battista are servants. Their expenses here will be covered, but each will receive a single payment of one hundred écus. Any compensation beyond that will be at your discretion."

Later that day, when Leonardo gave Salai the news, Salai was furious.

"I shall take this up with Mesnières myself!" he fumed.

"You can't argue with a king," Leonardo said.

"I haven't spent all these years working for you for one hundred écus!"

"Then take your inheritance now instead of later," Leonardo said.

"Do you mean that?"

Leonardo nodded. "Yes, if it will ease your anger about the one hundred écus."

"It will," Salai spat.

"I'll have the notary draw up the papers and give you the money."

"For how much?"

Salai's question stung Leonardo. Had it always been so for Salai? Had their many years together been only about the money? He spoke. "Three hundred florins."

"Done," Salai said, then walked away.

The next morning, King Francis stood transfixed before the three paintings in Leonardo's bedroom. "This is not only a viewing of your work, Leonardo," he finally said. "It's a glimpse into your mind and heart, and another realm I have only imagined until now."

"Thank you, Your Highness, but I'm still perfecting my *Mona Lisa*."

"Perfecting? Each of these paintings has already achieved a perfection unknown in all of France!" Francis exclaimed. He turned to face Leonardo. "Someday, your work will be on public display for everyone to see, to be inspired by, and to learn from." Francis wiped a tear from his cheek.

"I am honored, Your Highness."

"I have no word to describe my feelings. I suppose they are a mixture of joy, fascination, and admiration. God has truly blessed us with your presence here. Leonardo, I want you to help me create a legacy I can be proud of. Something that goes beyond my estates and palaces, most of which are inherited." He smiled. "These paintings could be part of that legacy."

"I am truly grateful."

Francis looked closely at the maestro. "I further believe that you and I will become close friends. So you will forgive me for asking what is wrong. I see sadness in your face."

Leonardo sighed. "Salai is gone. He left for Milan early this morning."

"You just arrived. Was he already unhappy?"

"He was unhappy with his circumstances. When I offered him the money he would have received upon my death, he took it."

"I'm sorry, Leonardo."

"He was never what I hoped he would be, so that's the end of it."

Within a year, Salai would be dead, killed in a duel.

Using only his right hand and arm, keeping his left arm pressed to his side, Leonardo struggled to adjust the easel on which the *Mona Lisa* rested. Francis reached out to assist him. Then the two men sat in chairs near the sunlit window.

"I see that you favor your left arm," the king said.

"I hoped that you wouldn't notice," Leonardo said. "I can't paint much with my left hand, although I can still draw with it."

"We will get you the best doctors. If they can't help you, then you don't have to paint anymore. Your drawings are a world unto themselves. They are beyond price, full of life and meaning."

Something else was on Leonardo's mind besides Salai's departure and his troublesome left arm. He had accepted the patronage of a king whose armies overran his homeland.

Back in Rome, when Francesco had challenged his decision to move to France, Leonardo had replied, "I am a practical man." But he had wondered ever since if he had taken practicality too far with the French and even earlier in his life, when working for Sforza and especially Cesare Borgia.

He decided to brave a question with the king.

"There is something I want to ask, Your Highness," Leonardo said.

"Then ask," Francis said.

"Why did your armies invade my country?"

Francis sighed. From the moment he told Henri de Mesnières to make Leonardo an offer, he knew this conversation would come one day. This was sooner than he thought, but it couldn't be avoided. While speaking with Leonardo, he would have to quell his own rage at the church in Rome and its agents in France. Still, he felt his face turning red. Leonardo noticed with alarm. Had he overstepped?

"We are speaking in complete confidence, Leonardo," Francis warned.

"Of course, Your Highness."

"Then I will tell you why." He took a moment to calm himself. "Do you know the nature of the church in France? Do you know the wealth it saps from my people and sends back to Rome? Do you know with what arrogance the church conducts its business in my homeland?"

"I have no knowledge of those things. I have lived in Italy all my life."

"The church in France and across Europe is a business. It's all about money. They make a mockery of Our Lord Jesus Christ, who removed the moneylenders from the temple. The French people give and the church takes. And what does the church do with our money? While the poor suffer, they cover everything in gold. While the peasants starve, they feast from plates of gold. Walk into any church and what do you see? Gold!"

Francis stood and began pacing angrily around Leonardo's room. "What benefits does the church provide to my people?" he asked, his voice rising. "The priests say, 'Have faith!' Will their lives be improved by faith alone? Not when they need good works, and bread. Does the church do good works for my people, or give them bread? It takes their money and sends it to Rome. It sells indulgences to the guilt-ridden and sends that money to Rome. Rome controls it all. They are sitting on more wealth than you can possibly imagine!"

"But why go to war?" Leonardo persisted.

"Because it was the only way to bring some kind of independence to the churches in France. To win the right to elect our own priests and church leaders without interference from Rome. And the right to tithe clerics for the money they collect from the French before they send it all to Rome."

Francis stopped near a window and gazed out. At the moment, the beauty of the Loire Valley was lost on him. "For years," he continued, "my uncle, King Louis, pressed the Holy See for these rights. For years, he was ignored or denied. When I took the throne, I knew what had been happening in my country. I had heard the arguments between my uncle and the bishops, archbishops, and cardinals. Before our eyes, the church had taken over France. My uncle knew that, and that is why he invaded Italy seventeen years ago."

Francis sat back down in his chair, took a deep breath, and wiped sweat off his brow with a handkerchief. "I'm sorry, Leonardo, but that is not what religion is supposed to be about. It's supposed to serve, not dominate! I will not be dominated, nor will I let France be dominated. That is why I overran your country—to force Rome to be fair to us. If I had to go to Rome and install my own pope, I was ready to do that too. And Leo knew it. That's why he brought you to Bologna. To soften me up and persuade me to reach a compromise."

Leonardo couldn't resist. "Well, it worked, didn't it?"

Surprised, Francis laughed out loud. Then he grew serious again. "I'm sorry we killed so many of your countrymen to achieve some measure of fairness from Rome. Do you think I enjoy killing?"

"Of course not."

"Neither do I enjoy watching my country squeezed of its wealth, year after year."

Without thinking, Leonardo put a hand on the young king's shoulder. "I understand everything. Your explanation has satisfied me completely. I have no need to discuss this ever again."

"Then let us move our chairs closer to your marvelous paintings. I want to study them more thoroughly."

They sat in companionable silence for a while before Francis spoke again.

"Several things about your *Mona Lisa* are enthralling to me," the king said. "You use an imaginary background with an aerial perspective. I have never seen that in a painting until now. And her eyes. How did you get those eyes and that smile?"

"I didn't have to do anything," Leonardo responded. "They presented themselves to me. Those *are* her eyes, and her smile."

He smiled bitterly. "It is the smile of my undoing. She could have saved me."

"So you were in love?"

"No, but someday I'll tell you what I know of her. It's still painful to discuss."

"*Ah, oui. Toujours la femme.*"

Leonardo stood, opened a window, and breathed the sweet autumn air. It was chilly, but a welcome change from the city odors of Rome.

"By the way," Francis said, "I have received many studies my agents in Italy made of your accomplishments, and I have decided to award you a pension of one thousand gold crowns a year. I am also appointing you First Painter, Engineer, and Architect to the Court of France."

"You heap rewards and honors on me, but there's not much that an old man like me can do anymore," Leonardo said.

"I will be content to enjoy the conversation of the most cultivated man alive," Francis said. "I have much to learn from you."

Leonardo sat down beside Francis once more. "But you are *my* teacher," he protested. "We will be like Aristotle and Alexander the Great, each learning from the other, although my knowledge will never approach that of Aristotle."

"Let us not indulge in false modesty, Leonardo."

"I am a kingdom divided against itself," Leonardo said.

"What do you mean by that?"

"I have spent so much time pursuing so many subjects that I am weakened and confused by my own curiosity."

Francis brightened. "Then you will be pleased to hear that my agents continually scour Europe for rare books and manuscripts. They buy whole collections and send them back to me.

Wait until you see my library. It is at your disposal. You won't have to pursue knowledge anymore. It will come to you."

Leonardo was truly humbled. All he could say was, "Thank you."

"I don't think Italy understands what treasures and cultural advances it possesses in the work you left behind," Francis mused. "But France will preserve them for you, and carry your breakthroughs in the arts and sciences even further. My agent in Milan is investigating the possibility of buying your *Last Supper* and shipping it here."

Now it was Leonardo's turn to laugh. "They would have to send the entire wall on which the fresco is painted! It's unthinkable. The trip would destroy it. The monks—especially the prior—would never stand for it. Someday I'll have to tell you a funny story about the prior."

Some days later, Francis and Leonardo sat on horseback at the top of a hill overlooking a stream that crossed a beautiful plain. Francis pointed to somewhere in the distance.

"The Château de Chambord will be my hunting lodge, in the exact center of France," he proclaimed.

"It's a palazzo, not a lodge," Leonardo laughed.

"But you are including rooms for dressing game?"

"Of course. I don't eat meat, but I won't deny it to others."

"How is the design progressing?" Francis wanted to know.

"Slowly. I'm designing a whole city around it, based on a plan I made for Milan that was never realized. Due to your uncle's invasion," he added drily.

"Tell me more about the city," the king prodded.

Leonardo continued. "We must dig canals so that various waterways emanating from the grounds of your château, like light from a star, will lead to streams and rivers in the region. The canals will accommodate fountains and a large lake for aquatic spectacles. They will also be used for irrigation of crops, street cleaning, and removal of rubbish."

Francis was impressed. "There won't be a city in Europe like it. Have you made plans to drain the Sologne marshes?"

"No. I need to survey the area further."

Not long after, Leonardo stood in the vast workshop of the palace with the king, his architects, and his engineers as they viewed a large-scale model of a massive château. Leonardo opened a box. "This is my small contribution to your château, Your Highness."

"He downplays his assistance, Your Highness," one of the architects protested. "Monsieur Léonard has helped us with the entire design of the structure."

Francis nodded, then watched as Leonardo inserted a double-helix staircase into the entrance foyer at the center of the model. The others oohed and aahed.

That afternoon, Leonardo and Francis walked in a hallway of the palace. "As with everything else you create, the staircase is brilliant," Francis said. "Oh, and you were right about *The Last Supper*. The trip to France would destroy it, so we'll let the Milanese keep it. But my troops will descend on them, should they abuse it," the king joked. "That and your *Mona Lisa* are probably the greatest paintings in the known world."

A few weeks later, Francis stood again before the trio of paintings in Leonardo's bedroom. Munching a croissant, the king looked thoughtfully at *St. John the Baptist* and the *Virgin and Child with St. Anne.*

"May I assume that Saint John and Saint Anne are each pointing to heaven?" Francis wanted to know.

"What does your intuition tell you?" Leonardo asked.

"The only thing I can think of is heaven," Francis said, leaning closer. "What else could it be?"

"What else do you think it can be?"

"Whatever Saint John points to causes him to smile with serenity and certainty. I think he points to something better than man's lot on earth."

"Better how?"

"Spiritually better, I must assume, because of his otherworldly smile."

"Good," Leonardo answered, satisfied. "I painted it that way, if a bit mysteriously. As I have told you, I believe to be true only what I can observe to be true. I leave a lot of room for viewers to interpret my paintings as they wish."

Leonardo took a croissant from the table and stood beside Francis. "As for something better spiritually for man, I think it does exist, and it has to do with man's divine nature."

"Man's divine nature?" Francis exclaimed. "My God! To have the audacity to paint such a thing!" His face changed, and he spoke softly, as if to himself. "Not of an angel's divine nature, but of our own? Ourselves, and everyone we see?"

Leonardo smiled. He remembered the day, years ago, when Francesco had experienced a similar revelation.

"No painter," Francis was saying, "and few philosophers have ventured into this subject matter with any…"

"Certainty?" Leonardo offered. "That's understandable, given that most of them, dependent on the church's patronage, are careful to walk the straight and narrow dogmatic line."

"But to view men as having an independent, yet divine nature! Why have so few hinted at this?"

"Fear," said Leonardo. "Only fear, that makes men silence what is in their hearts to say. I've spent most of my working life saying it to friends in private. My words have fallen mostly on deaf ears."

"What a burden to carry," Francis added.

"But when they see my paintings…"

"Yes?"

"Then they are in *my* world."

Leonardo picked up a human skull from a shelf and turned it over in his hands.

"I know that something exists beyond death, in another dimension. And it's not oblivion."

"Go on," Francis urged.

"I have been trying most of my life to observe it and put it into words or images. As a child, I asked a beekeeper why I could not see God."

"And you never gave up?" asked Francis.

"I was fool enough to think I could find the answer. Without this search, I would have been just another painter, trying to find commissions."

Chapter Twenty-Eight

NOTHING

Three years passed during which Leonardo worked for King Francis on various architectural and hydraulic designs, as well as elaborate and magnificent stage sets and fireworks extravaganzas *pour les grandes fêtes*—important occasions at the palace, such as the marriages of the king's close relatives. They occupied Leonardo without putting too much mental or physical strain on him.

He had not yet entered his dotage; his mind remained sharp and clear. But by the early months of 1519, his left shoulder was causing him great pain. The king's doctors could do nothing for him. Leonardo often joked that he would pay to have it cut off.

One day in his bedroom, he stood in front of the *Mona Lisa*, clutching several fine brushes and a palette in his right hand, painting with his left and smiling through his pain. Driven to finish the portrait, he was spending a small amount of each day working on it. For a time, he had tried painting with his right hand, but it wasn't the same, and he was forced to paint over the work he had done.

He stepped back and studied the portrait intensely. After some minutes, he took a very fine brush and put a tiny dab of ocher on it. Holding his breath, he applied the paint to the canvas, inside the iris of Lisa's left eye, slowly, gently, and carefully, intimating an object reflected there.

He exhaled and stepped back again, surveying the entire work in detail, scanning for flaws. Switching to a different brush, he dipped it into the ultramarine on his palette and applied it to a highlight in Lisa's hair. Then he looked at the painting for a very long time. Suddenly, he laughed.

Leonardo's laughter became stronger and louder. He put down his palette and brushes and sat in a chair in front of his Lisa. His laughter turned to sobs and wails. His body shook.

The sound of running footsteps approached, and Francesco rushed into the room. He took in the scene with dismay.

"What's wrong, Maestro?"

He saw Leonardo rub his shoulder; he saw the brushes and the wet oils on the palette.

"You've been painting!" Francesco scolded. "What did the doctors tell you? They warned you that—"

"This is the first work I have ever truly finished," Leonardo said, now perfectly calm.

"Finished? You finished Lisa?"

Leonardo beamed. "It's as if I have emerged from my mother's womb," he said. "I'm ready to return to something greater."

Francesco heard the hope in the maestro's voice. He wished he felt the same.

From that day on, Leonardo was constantly ill and progressively more so. At least he had finished the *Mona Lisa*, the most precious of his trio. He was satisfied to let the three paintings stand as his legacy, and if Francis wanted to purchase them later from Francesco and make them France's legacy, all the better.

Francesco would be Leonardo's heir. He could decide when the time came.

Thoughts of death increasingly crossed his mind. One day, he wrote in his notebook:

Just as a well-filled day brings blessed sleep, so a well-employed life brings a blessed death.

He lost all motivation to pursue anything but idle doodling with mathematical abstractions. His viewpoint on the soul had changed. He no longer pursued further insights. He wrote in his notebook:

It is with the greatest reluctance that the soul leaves the body, and I think that its sorrow and lamentations are not without cause.

By now, Leonardo was writing about his own soul.

One day, he sat at his desk as a notary watched him sign his will, then applied his wax seal to the document. Francesco stood nearby, glumly watching.

"Why is this necessary?" he asked. "You're going to live many more years, Leonardo. Like your father."

Leonardo looked impassively at Francesco. "There is nothing more certain than death, and nothing more uncertain than the day and the hour."

Early one morning, a few weeks later, a side door of the Château de Cloux flew open, disturbing a robin on a nearby tree branch.

Out dashed Battista. He raced into the stable and burst out a few moments later, cracking a whip over the flanks of a mare.

Leonardo had been fading all night. Francesco stayed by his side. He knew the end was near, and he couldn't bear it. As Leonardo's breathing became more labored, Francesco tried to comfort him. "Battista has gone to fetch the king," he said. "He will be here soon."

Leonardo was in a fevered sleep, dreaming once more of the deluge. He saw two figures waving from a prow of a boat. Francis and Francesca. Their mouths opened as if they were yelling but emitted no sound. The boat moved away and faded from sight. A wave the size of a mountain rose up, crested, and was about to bury him when he heard Francesco's voice. He opened his eyes to see his loving friend looking down at him, his face a mixture of grief and fear.

"You were calling me, Maestro," Francesco said.

"Just another bad dream," Leonardo answered weakly. "They come all the time now."

"I wish I could do something more for you."

"You've been doing more for me for ten years. Long enough. You've earned a rest."

"It has all been out of love."

Leonardo smiled and reached for Francesco's hand. "We've been through a lot."

"I'd do it again."

"You might not survive it a second time. I wouldn't."

Francesco laughed.

Leonardo turned serious. "I have left you almost everything."

"Don't talk about that now," Francesco insisted.

"I must. Those thieves…my stepbrothers. Don't let them challenge my will. Use my lawyers in Florence."

"Whatever you wish. I'm grateful to have worked for you and learned from you all these years. You have made me a painter."

"I hope I have also made you a searcher."

Francesco nodded. "I'll continue your work on the soul, Leonardo. But I don't know if I'll find more answers than you."

"Just keep asking questions."

For a while, neither man spoke. The only sound was Leonardo's breathing.

"I'm going soon where no one wants to go," Leonardo said, "but where everyone wishes they could see ahead of time. We know so little about the most important things. And we kill each other over pieces of dirt."

"I know, Leonardo. When will that end?"

"You sound like me."

"After ten years, I'd be surprised if I didn't."

"Please…organize my notes."

"I have already begun. There are thousands of pages, which will become many volumes."

"Good. They won't be lost. That's something. Where is Francis?"

"He will be here very soon."

"He should hurry. Or he will miss final performance of Leonardo of Vinci."

"Stop, Leonardo!" Francesco cried. "I can't imagine losing you!" His voice broke in sobs.

Battista had arrived at Château d'Amboise, the palace of the French king. The sentries knew him and let him through, as did the guards at the entrance. Once inside the palace, Battista explained to more guards that he had an urgent message for the king from Château de Cloux.

Carrying a sealed letter, he was escorted to the double doors of the royal conference room, where he spoke briefly with one of the king's secretaries. As the doors opened, Battista caught a glimpse of King Francis at the head of a table filled with seated ministers.

"Who dares to disturb this meeting?" one of the ministers asked indignantly.

"His servant apologizes, Excellency, but someone has brought a letter from the Château de Cloux. For the king's eyes only."

"Where is it?" Francis said, rising from his chair. "Bring it immediately!"

Moments later, Battista stood just inside the doors as Francis read the letter. "We will continue tomorrow," the king announced. Ignoring the looks from the ministers, he rushed out of the room with Battista close behind. Soon he was galloping toward the manor on a powerful stallion, accompanied by ten mounted escorts.

Reaching the courtyard of the Château de Cloux, Francis quickly dismounted, ran through the doors, and took the stairs two at a time to Leonardo's room. He nearly collided with the royal physician, who bowed formally to his king.

"He has been asking for you, Your Highness," the physician said. "It won't be long."

Grief welled up in Francis's throat.

Inside Leonardo's room, the parish priest had just finished saying the last rites. Leonardo—cheeks hollow, breathing shallow, eyes half-closed—looked as if he might disappear into his bed. Both the priest and Francesco bowed and left the room. Francis and Leonardo were alone.

Francis sat on the chair where the priest had been and said only, "Leonardo."

Leonardo opened his eyes fully and smiled. "My friend. You've come for my finale. I hope it will not disappoint."

"Leonardo, you have yet to disappoint me."

Leonardo tried to sit up.

"Save your energy," Francis urged, placing a hand gently on Leonardo's chest.

The king looked lovingly at the artist. "It pains me, like a son viewing his father, to see you confined to your bed. How are you feeling?"

"I have failed," Leonardo said bitterly. "All of my works have come to nothing."

"That is not true!" Francis protested. He tried to lighten the moment. "And I will sign a royal edict to that effect."

"A man should not have to live this long without gaining what he seeks," Leonardo wheezed.

"I have tried to provide everything you required," Francis said, mystified. Had he failed his friend?

"You have been so kind. But you mistake my meaning."

Leonardo paused, gathering his thoughts and his strength.

"When I was six years old," he finally said, "I picked up a bone in the forest. I wanted to know what makes life. It was a foolish question, but I kept asking. I never finished anything except my Lisa."

"The answer is simple, my friend. God makes life."

Leonardo sighed. "I have made my confession. Now I can speak freely. I was never satisfied with 'God makes life.' How does God make life? Why?"

He tried and failed to take a deep breath.

"I should have painted without questions. Instead, I finished little and pleased few."

"You have pleased many, Leonardo!" Francis exclaimed. "You have inspired and enlightened all who have seen your work. And we need you to do more."

"It's over," Leonardo said. "The play is done."

Moments passed. Tears fell from Francis's eyes. Leonardo turned his head to look at the *Mona Lisa* and smiled weakly.

"At least I finished her," he said. "I have done with Lisa Gherardini. She never told me her secret. Now whoever sees her must suffer, as I did."

He coughed for a long time and spit into a handkerchief.

"Why do you say that?" Francis asked.

"She was the closest I came to knowing." His eyes shone. "She knows, Francis! Who we really are and where we go. I spent my life trying to find out and she wouldn't tell me!" Tears welled in his eyes. "I could see the many times she died. She dove in deep oceans. I knew that much."

"I don't understand."

Leonardo's eyes pleaded with Francis, "Will you try to find her? Francesco tried and failed. I don't even know if she is still alive. Find her, and tell her!" He fumbled for Francis's hand.

"Tell her what?"

"That I will forgive her, if she tells you. Someone must carry on, because I have failed. My life has been wasted."

"Your life has not been wasted! I will find Lisa, if she still lives, and tell her what you have said."

Leonardo squeezed Francis's hand with surprising strength. Then he said something truly astounding: "Follow the finger." He looked toward *St. John the Baptist*.

Francis had spent hours before that painting. For the thousandth time, he saw the finger pointing to...what? Where?

It hit him like a thunderclap. "That's not really John the Baptist, is it?" Francis asked. "It's you!"

Leonardo attempted a laugh, which turned into a rattling cough. When he could breathe again, he said simply, "Now you perceive the painting correctly."

Francis was not in the mood for praise. He wanted to *know*. He had always wanted to know, ever since he was a child, reading voraciously in his father's library while others went to parties. His friend was dying, but Francis asked, "To what are you pointing?"

"To a better state for man," Leonardo said. "Peace with himself, and with others. A state where man knows the answers."

"And what are the answers?" Francis demanded.

"Beyond that, I have nothing."

"So you—not John the Baptist, but you—are not pointing to heaven after all?"

"No one knows where heaven is. Though we spend enough on priests to get there." Leonardo had spent a small fortune on his own funeral, which he would never see. For a moment, he was annoyed, then overcome by grief.

His body was struggling, but his mind remained lucid. "Something lies beyond the flesh," he said.

Now Francis was annoyed. "Just like Lisa, you know more than you're saying," the king insisted. "As you said, you have made your confession. No inquisitors, priests, or popes can touch you now. Tell me! What is the soul? Don't leave me with nothing!"

"Nothing *is* the answer," Leonardo said, as if to himself. "About the soul, I am still in the dark cave of my childhood. Except for this. It's all so simple."

The old maestro smiled like a child. The unfinished commissions, the disastrous losses of his Milanese masterpieces, his precious *Anghiari* mural in Florence—all fell away in an instant. "Among the great things of importance, Nothing is the most important."

Francis was thoroughly confused. Had Leonardo lost his mind? Was this the end? He blurted, "Nothing? What is nothing?"

"The unseen, unheard, unsmelled, unfelt unobservable," Leonardo said. "The divine soul of man. Pure joy. Not your soul. Yours and everyone's. You don't *have* a soul. You *are* a soul."

Leonardo's words, halting just minutes earlier, flowed like a river.

"Go on, my friend," Francis said, his face full of wonder.

"My beloved son, you are not of this earth," Leonardo said. "None of us are. We are all outside time and space. You stretch back into the past and forward into the future. You and I will continue! I will complete many masterpieces. You will be king of many lands."

Francis was elated and devastated at the same moment. He wept with joy and sorrow.

"John the Baptist had the light. Look into his eyes."

"Have you seen that light before?" Francis wanted to know.

"Just now, in your eyes," Leonardo said. "Many years ago, in a child's eyes on the Ponte Vecchio. In the eyes of lovers, and those who are truly inspired."

"What is the light?"

"It is eternity. Man calls it the soul. I call it Nothing. I can't paint it. It can't be seen."

"But you did paint it, Leonardo! Your paintings showed it to me."

"And now you're trying to comfort me," Leonardo said.

"No, I'm not."

"One thing is certain. Science cannot discover such things. But man can."

Leonardo coughed, long and deep, then sighed a rattling sigh.

"I pass my torch to you and Francesco," he said. "He has given his life to me and would sacrifice it for mine, if he could. He asked for nothing and was always loyal. Take care of him."

"I'll see to his well-being for as long as he lives," Francis pledged.

"I'm giving him almost everything. But what if my paintings are worthless?"

Francesco laughed. "They will only increase in value."

"Tastes change."

"Your paintings are beyond tastes and fashions. As long as men breathe, their hearts beat, and their eyes see, they will value your work. One day, it will be priceless."

"Perhaps they will cause others to seek answers I couldn't find."

"Then you have made a difference," Francis said. "And your life has not been wasted." Once more, he turned to gaze at the paintings. "I sent my agents to Italy to discover what others have learned from your works. Many had the same experience."

Almost whispering, Leonardo asked, "And what was it?"

"They saw the truth you spoke of. They saw who we really are. The life of the soul beyond this world. The ultimate truth."

"Then it's certain," Leonardo said. "The truth cannot be hidden."

And with that, he was gone.

Francis cried out, and Francesco, the doctor, and the priest came in. Francesco broke down. The doctor confirmed the death and muttered, "A great loss." The priest gave a final blessing.

Once the doctor and the priest had left, Francis asked Francesco, "Can you fulfill Leonardo's request and find Lisa Gherardini?"

"I have already found her," Francesco said. "In Florence. She wouldn't tell me anything, and I didn't have the heart to tell him." He looked toward Leonardo's body. "Whatever Leonardo felt she knew, Lisa will take to her grave."

"No matter," the king said. "In his paintings, he told us what he knew. If one will only look."

Francis put an arm around Francesco's shoulders. "Come for a walk in the gardens. It will do us both good."

On a sunny afternoon in the Tuscan hills, an intelligent and delighted seven-year-old boy lay amid the ferns and flowers on the forest floor. A nearby bird sang in a tree. He smiled, then laughed in glee. His eyes glowed with happiness. He had found the secret.

Acknowledgments

I would like to thank Robert Barbera, whose unflagging support of this book is just one example of a lifetime he has spent educating Americans on the importance of Italian and Italian-American cultural contributions to the improvement of the human condition and the expansion of man's awareness. I would also like to thank my literary agent, Sherry Robb, of the Robb Company, for her constant encouragement and her invaluable critique that helped me make it a better novel. My grateful appreciation goes to Professor Constance Moffat for commenting on the manuscript and contributing the foreword. Additionally, I very much appreciate the encouragement and praise from both Alberto di Mauro, the former director of the Italian Cultural Institute in Los Angeles, as well as his former deputy director, Michela Magri, who both took the time to read the screenplay version of this book. Additionally, my readings of some of the world's great writers—Leo Tolstoy, Joseph Conrad, Anton Chekhov, and Erich Maria Remarque—have helped me, with their honesty and clarity, lay the keel for this vessel with which I embark on my maiden voyage across the blank white pages of my first novel.

In researching Leonardo, I relied on many sources, including over fifty books (both nonfiction and fiction) culled from both public and university libraries; hundreds of internet searches and articles; and several documentary films. Senior to all that information were the teachers I've had over the years. Some of their names are not even dimly recalled, yet all gave me the spirit of inquiry and the viewpoint that I could find out whatever

I wanted to know if I only had the patience to search for it. Specifically, a history teacher in junior high school posed us a question every week for which the obscure answers could only be found through painstaking research in local libraries. I warmed to the challenge and never failed to find what he required of us. He was the first teacher to instill research skills in me.

However, my late mother, Jeannette, a writer and researcher herself, was the first to imbue me with that spirit and to recognize and validate my writing talent. My late father, Irv, a sculptor and writer, taught me to look and to see beauty. My elementary school teacher, Charles Quigley, praised and encouraged my fiction and even staged a scene I wrote for a play in front of my fourth-grade class. I appreciate my junior high and high school papers for printing my efforts as a cub reporter. I want to thank the Boosters Club of Palisades High School in Los Angeles for bestowing an award on me for my writing when I graduated, and for the *Analecta* literary magazine for publishing examples of my literary output during those years. All these encouragements meant a lot to me.

Later, at the University of California, Santa Cruz, two professors, William Hitchcock and Mary Holmes, made history and art history literally come alive. In so doing, they gave me a critical grounding in Western civilization and art that has tremendously informed the writing of this book. When I became a sculptor and an art major on the campus, several brilliant artist-professors gave their time, attention, and care to me and drew out of me my own creative sensibilities as a sculptor, without which I could never have fully understood Leonardo and his creations. Gurdon Woods, Don Weygandt, Fred Hunnicutt, Jack Zajac, and Doug McClellan are all very much appreciated for their encouragement, support, and expert critiquing.

ACKNOWLEDGMENTS

Beyond that, I credit and acknowledge the University of California, Santa Cruz, overall with providing a superlative learning and growing environment for my young mind and heart—complete with unqualified intellectual and artistic freedom granted to me from literally every quarter of the campus. For the staff and professors there, no request of mine was ever too large or too small. I found my intellectual and creative selves there, in an environment where they could develop and flourish without restraints of any kind. Where else could I have had my first stage play produced, my first sculpture exhibit shown, and my first film unspooled for an audience, all in my sophomore year? For the University's encouragement and inspiration, I'm eternally grateful.

Finally, to all those researchers and writers of Vinciana who have come before me, you have my everlasting gratitude for giving me an understanding of this very great man. As we UC Santa Cruz alumni would say, "*Fiat lux!*" ("Let there be light!")

—Peter David Myers

About the Author

Peter has sold, written for hire, or optioned ten theatrical feature scripts, and has done a number of rewrites for indie film and TV producers. Two short films, a stage play, and numerous TV public service announcements have been produced from his scripts.

His produced projects include nine *Chapters in Black American History*, the drama/comedy *The Pickup*, his half-hour suspense drama, *Double Cross*, as well as *Speak To The World*, a pilot for an interview show.

One of Peter's comedy feature scripts won an Honorable Mention at the Thunderbird International Film Festival Script Competition.

Peter has judged scripts for UCLA's Master of Fine Arts Screenwriting Showcase and has been a regular panelist at the West Coast Writers Conference. His advice to screenwriters is part of Tarcher/Penguin's anthology, *NOW WRITE! Screenwriting: Exercises by Today's Best Screenwriters, Teachers and Consultants*.

NOW AVAILABLE FROM THE MENTORIS PROJECT

America's Forgotten Founding Father
A Novel Based on the Life of Filippo Mazzei
by Rosanne Welch

A. P. Giannini—The People's Banker
by Francesca Valente

Christopher Columbus: His Life and Discoveries
by Mario Di Giovanni

Fermi's Gifts
A Novel Based on the Life of Enrico Fermi
by Kate Fuglei

God's Messenger
The Astounding Achievements of Mother Cabrini
A Novel Based on the Life of Mother Frances X. Cabrini
by Nicole Gregory

Harvesting the American Dream
A Novel Based on the Life of Ernest Gallo
by Karen Richardson

Marconi and His Muses
A Novel Based on the Life of Guglielmo Marconi
by Pamela Winfrey

NOW AVAILABLE FROM THE MENTORIS PROJECT

Saving the Republic
A Novel Based on the Life of Marcus Cicero
by Eric D. Martin

Soldier, Diplomat, Archaeologist
A Novel Based on the Bold Life of Louis Palma di Cesnola
by Peg A. Lamphier

COMING IN 2018 FROM THE MENTORIS PROJECT

A Novel Based on the Life of Alessandro Volta
A Novel Based on the Life of Angelo Dundee
A Novel Based on the Life of Filippo Brunelleschi
A Novel Based on the Life of Giuseppe Verdi
A Novel Based on the Life of Henry Mancini
A Novel Based on the Life of Maria Montessori
A Novel Based on the Life of Publius Cornelius Scipio
A Novel Based on the Life of Saint Thomas Aquinas

Fulfilling the Promise of California: An Anthology
of Essays on the Italian American Experience in California

FUTURE TITLES FROM THE MENTORIS PROJECT

A Novel Based on the Life of Amerigo Vespucci
A Novel Based on the Life of Andrea Palladio
A Novel Based on the Life of Antonin Scalia
A Novel Based on the Life of Antonio Meucci
A Novel Based on the Life of Buzzie Bavasi
A Novel Based on the Life of Cesare Becaria
A Novel Based on the Life of Federico Fellini
A Novel Based on the Life of Frank Capra
A Novel Based on the Life of Galileo Galilei
A Novel Based on the Life of Giovanni Andrea Doria
A Novel Based on the Life of Giovanni di Bicci de' Medici
A Novel Based on the Life of Giuseppe Garibaldi
A Novel Based on the Life of Guido Monaco
A Novel Based on the Life of Harry Warren
A Novel Based on the Life of John Cabot
A Novel Based on the Life of Judge John Sirica
A Novel Based on the Life of Leonard Covello
A Novel Based on the Life of Luca Pacioli
A Novel Based on the Life of Mario Andretti
A Novel Based on the Life of Mario Cuomo
A Novel Based on the Life of Niccolo Machiavelli
A Novel Based on the Life of Peter Rodino
A Novel Based on the Life of Pietro Belluschi
A Novel Based on the Life of Robert Barbera
A Novel Based on the Life of Saint Augustine of Hippo
A Novel Based on the Life of Saint Francis of Assisi
A Novel Based on the Life of Vince Lombardi

For more information on these titles and
The Mentoris Project, please visit
www.mentorisproject.org.

Printed in Great Britain
by Amazon